DOCTOR NEVER DOES

D0234295

'Nurses are supposed to provide tender loving care—keep your interest strictly professional and leave other people to get on with their own lives.' Dr Craig Dean's harsh words caused resentment to burn in the breast of Sister Rosemary Miller. So much for trying to help with the doctor's personal problems—from now on she would confine herself to ulcers, wounds and injections!

Hazel Fisher is a trained psychiatric nurse but has also worked on medical and surgical wards in general hospitals. She draws on her own nursing experiences to provide the background for her novels, supplemented where necessary by careful research. She is half-Geordie but has spent most of her life in Sussex, and now lives in a pretty little village nestling at the foot of the South Downs. She enjoys reading and writing Doctor Nurse Romances, and believes they educate, as well as entertain the reader, and provide some much-needed escapism.

Hazel Fisher has written fourteen other Doctor Nurse Romances, the most recent being *Calling Dr Haldane*, *The Heart Specialist* and *Nurse Isobel's Dream*.

DOCTOR NEVER DOES

BY

HAZEL FISHER

MILLS & BOON LIMITED
ETON HOUSE 18–24 PARADISE ROAD
RICHMOND SURREY TW9 1SR

*First published in Great Britain 1987
by Mills & Boon Limited*

© Hazel Fisher 1987

*Australian copyright 1987
Philippine copyright 1987*

ISBN 0 263 75809 5

Set in 11 on 11½ pt Linotron Times
03–0987–48,150

*Photoset by Rowland Phototypesetting Limited
Bury St Edmunds, Suffolk
Made and printed in Great Britain by
William Collins Sons & Co. Limited, Glasgow*

CHAPTER ONE

'HERE we are, then, Sister, that's the notes on old Mrs Honeysett. She isn't what she was, poor soul. Oh, and she'll likely give you a few eggs.' Gwen Sayers, the perky grey-haired receptionist, placed a bulky folder in front of the new district nursing Sister.

Rosemary Miller smiled, her grey eyes twinkling. 'Do *all* the patients provide us with free meals? This is only my third day and I've been inundated with offers of food!' She ticked off the items on her fingers. 'Mrs Putland gave me a home-made pork pie. The Fairleys offered me a rabbit . . . Who else? Oh yes, Mrs Taylor. She didn't actually give me anything, but she recommended the goats' milk.'

'You'll not get anything from *her*,' Gwen said darkly. 'She'll make you pay for the goats' milk, though I don't say as it's not nutritious.'

'I'll bear that in mind,' Rosemary said lightly, beginning to work through the bursting folder. Then a frown creased her wide brow. 'Is this the right patient, Gwen? She's ninety. The woman I met this morning was in her fifties, I should imagine.'

'Oh, that'll be *young* Mrs Honeysett you saw, then.' Undismayed, Gwen swiftly removed the folder from Rosemary's surprised grasp and substituted another, even thicker one.

'Is young Mrs Honeysett in her fifties?' Rosemary asked weakly.

'No! She's sixty-seven, though she doesn't look it, I daresay. She dyes her hair,' Gwen went on in an undertone, and Rosemary hastily suppressed a laugh. 'she's *old* Mrs Honeysett's daughter-in-law and they don't get on. Never did.'

'She's got a nasty leg ulcer and she doesn't seem to have consulted the doctor recently.'

'She used to come regular, then she fell out with the young doctor and hardly comes at all now.' Gwen was a mine of information, though she seemed to be rather a gossip. At least she was friendly to a foreigner!

It wasn't easy coming from an urban practice to a rural one, particularly when it involved a switch from the industrial Midlands to the heart of Ashdown Forest in Sussex. Perhaps 'culture shock' was too strong an expression, but certainly Rosemary found it hard to adapt to the more leisurely pace of country life. Mentally she shrugged. When all was said and done, a patient here was no different from a patient anywhere else.

She glanced across at the spry figure of Gwen Sayers. 'Perhaps when you have time, you can go through the list of patients with me. You're bound to know more of their background and ways than there is in the notes. This Mrs Primrose Cole, for instance. She——'

'Ah, that's old Granny Cole—lives at The Five Wishes. Dear old soul, she is.'

A smiled lurked in Rosemary's eyes. 'I'm sure she is, but what's wrong with her? She had my predecessor calling every week for months! It isn't at all clear from the notes exactly what Sister Pearson did for her.'

Gwen looked surprised. 'She didn't do anything much, except get her a nice cuppa, see that she was warm enough in winter, that sort of thing.'

Rosemary bit back the reply she wanted to make. Probably the old woman had no one else, but it certainly seemed a waste of a trained nurse's time. Guard your tongue, Rosemary, she told herself. Give yourself a few weeks before you try to change the habits of years.

'There, that's my list for tomorrow.' She sat back, idly brushing away a strand of flaxen hair that persisted in creeping out of her neat bun.

Gwen's eyes followed the movement. 'It's funny you being fair. Dr Dean *will* be surprised,' she commented. 'When he heard your name was Rosemary, he said you must be an exotic brunette. I suppose he's right—it *does* sound like a brunette name, somehow.'

'I'm sorry if Dr Dean's going to be disappointed!' Rosemary chuckled.

'Well, *he* might be, but Lyn Abbott won't,' Gwen commented dourly.

'Oh yes, the evening receptionist—you've mentioned her before. When do I meet her.'

'I shouldn't be in any hurry if I were you. It isn't everybody who takes to her, though she knows her stuff. She used to be a nurse before she married and she helps out at the clinic sometimes. But after young Steven came along . . . Well, I mustn't stand here gossiping.' Gwen hurried away, making Rosemary feel guilty at having delayed her.

She felt a mild curiosity about Lyn Abbott, but

no doubt all would be revealed sooner or later.

She tidied her desk, then left the old creeper-covered house. It was a warm evening for early October, with only a faint hint of autumn. October in the Weald would be beautiful, she mused as she walked the few hundred yards to the village where she lived in a small cottage.

Hurstfield was a thriving village, almost a town, really, though it lacked a really good restaurant. The nearest one was at Haywards Heath, and Rosemary missed the urban amenities more than she would have believed possible.

One thing she did not miss was Alec Scott. At least, she told herself she didn't. Her fine grey eyes clouded, and she narrowly missed bumping into a man coming from the opposite direction.

For one anguished moment she believed she had conjured him up, that it was Alec, came to tell her that he really *did* love her.

Then the hope died, and the eagerness faded from her face. It was a stranger, tall and casually dressed, but he appeared to know her. As she was in her district nurse's uniform, that was hardly surprising.

'Sister Miller?' The fair-haired man held out his hand, and Rosemary took it, his commanding presence hard to resist. 'I'm Dr Dean—Craig Dean. I'm sorry we haven't met before, I've been at a conference.'

Rosemary had half suspected that he was the 'young doctor' as Gwen called him, and she smiled, her face lighting up. He didn't look as stern and forbidding as his uncle, old Dr Tunstall, thank heavens.

In fact, he was decidedly attractive, though his features could best be described as craggy rather than handsome. Rather long, untidy fair hair and sleepy-looking pale blue eyes completed the picture. His handshake was firm and welcoming, and Rosemary decided she liked Dr Dean. If the fact that she was fair rather than dark displeased him, then she was genuinely sorry!

They strolled companionably the last few steps towards the cottage. Craig Dean was very tall and made even Rosemary feel petite and delicate, though she was tall herself and built on generous lines. Dr Tunstall had told her he was glad she was sturdy, because too many nurses looked as if a mere puff of wind would knock them over!

She couldn't help wondering if Lyn Abbott was well built, too, though why the woman should creep into her thoughts she had no idea. Perhaps it was something Gwen had let drop earlier, about Lyn and the young doctor being 'bosom pals', as she put it.

The thought was no sooner there than it vanished again and they were at the small, neat end-of-terrace cottage.

Dr Dean seemed inclined to linger, and Rosemary hesitatingly invited him in for a coffee. Quite *why* she hesitated, she wasn't sure. Perhaps it was the effect those sleepy blue eyes had on her.

Alec's eyes were blue as well, but there the resemblance ended. Angry with herself for letting her thoughts stray towards Alec, she led the way inside the cheerful little cottage.

As with many buildings of that age, its front door opened directly on to the sitting-room, but that was its only drawback, she felt. In her eyes it was everything else that a country cottage should be, down to the roses around the door. There was even a strand or two of honeysuckle winding its way up the rickety fence in the back garden. After city dwelling, it was heaven. And it was her own, as she'd declined the small council house which had been offered. Here at least she had a little privacy.

The ceilings were low and, once inside, the doctor seemed to fill the sitting-room.

With a murmured request that he should make himself at home, Rosemary escaped to the tiny, very basic kitchen. When she returned with two mugs of coffee, she found he'd taken her at her word. He was sprawled in the only armchair, long muscular legs stretched out in front of him, eyes half closed.

Something like shock hit her at the sight of a man in her home again, invading her privacy, smiling his way into her heart . . .

The doctor *did* smile at her entrance, rising to take the tray from her suddenly shaking hands. Once she was seated on the small overstuffed settee, he settled himself in the chair, long-fingered hands clasped around the insulated mug.

'Would you like some cake, doctor? Or I've a few digestive biscuits if you would prefer,' Her voice sounded strained, artificial, and she cleared her throat, hoping she wasn't catching an autumn cold.

He declined her offer. 'I'm dining out later. The coffee is fine for now.' He had a lazy, slightly crooked smile which Rosemary found endearing.

While they drank the coffee, Dr Dean filled her in with a few details of the practice and the area, and she mentally stored away the information. She had a retentive memory, fortunately, for the information came thick and fast.

She gathered, among other things, that the practice area was bigger than she had at first thought.

'Your northern boundary is at the Fairleys' farm,' he explained, waving a hand vaguely in a northward direction.

'I've met them,' she affirmed, recalling the family of six children. Apart from the children, there were numerous cats and a rather overweight dachshund. Then there was the children's pet goat . . .

'Did you meet the goat?' His eyes laughed at her.

'Yes. I think it liked me!'

'Be careful,' he warned. 'If the Fairleys think you're good with animals, they'll be seeking your advice on all kinds of veterinary problems!'

Rosemary broached the subject of Mrs Cole, pointing out that she could see no reason why her predecessor had called so often. 'Do you want me to fit her in every week, Doctor? I'll try, of course, but I can't see——'

His good humour faded abruptly. 'I certainly don't want you to "fit her in", as you put it! If it's inconvenient, forget it. One of the auxiliaries can visit.'

Rosemary pursed her lips. Dr Dean was going to be difficult, perhaps more so than his irascible uncle. 'I shall be happy to call on her, Doctor, but I need to know *why*,' she pointed out calmly.

They traded glances, then Craig Dean's lazy smile broke out again. 'I can see we're going to have some interesting disagreements, Sister!'

She smiled back. 'I certainly don't see myself as a

handmaiden to the doctor! I'm not one of those forelock-touching women who unquestioningly obey the orders of their superiors simply because they *are* superiors!'

'No, ma'am!' Dr Dean sketched a salute, the smile still hovering about his mouth. Evidently he was used to getting his own way, turning on the charm when he could not achieve his ends by other means. Well, he had more than met his match! Rosemary found herself looking forward to working with the man. It was a challenge.

She was about to make some remark about it, but he forestalled her, his question bringing sadness to her eyes. Yet the question was innocent enough. He couldn't know the pain that remembering caused.

'What brings you to Hurstfield, Sister? It seems rather a drastic move.'

His gaze was watchful now, the blue eyes no longer sleepy, and she flushed. 'Yes, I suppose it was,' she agreed. 'I—well, I needed a change. I have an aunt in the Haywards Heath area and——'

'A desire for change?' he broke in. 'Is that your only reason?'

Taken aback, Rosemary couldn't think straight for a moment. 'Should there be another reason, doctor? A deprived inner-city area isn't a place for an extended stay,' she pointed out. 'I stayed nearly three years.'

'So you did,' he mused, staring down into his coffee mug. 'It just struck me as odd that you should come all the way down to the south.'

'I was born in Eastbourne,' said Rosemary level-ly. His persistence was beginning to annoy her and she wondered at the reason behind it. Clearly the doctor was not merely being inquisitive. 'It's an attractive place to live—if you're over sixty,' she added, with a trace of asperity. 'I prefer to work with families, teenagers and so on. It's more rewarding to have a mixed bag of patients rather than ninety per cent retired folk.'

He nodded. 'For some, perhaps. You like children?'

Her face lit up. 'Yes, I do. Nothing gives me more pleasure than restoring a child to health. And feeling that I've given support to the family, of course.'

Pleased that the conversation had veered away from personal matters, Rosemary relaxed, even offering Dr Dean a second cup of coffee.

He declined, then yawned and stretched, lithe muscles rippling beneath the worn checked shirt.

Against her will, Rosemary's gaze was drawn to him. Of course he did not resemble Alec, really. He was taller and not so broad-shouldered, fair instead of dark, and a country healer instead of a tough, high-powered businessman. Yet . . . It crossed her mind that the sleepy-eyed doctor could also be tough and uncompromising.

His eyes met hers, and, confused and embarrassed, she sprang up. 'I'll take your cup, Doctor.'

A smile tugged at the corner of his mouth, as if he'd been aware of her scrutiny. Yet she hadn't really been staring at him. Or if she had, it was Alec Scott she was seeing, the man she had once foolishly loved.

The man she still loved, she amended, carrying

the tray into the dark little kitchen. Alec was a womaniser, charming but weak, unable to resist an unmistakable invitation from any attractive woman. She was a fool to yearn for him, to dwell on what might have been.

'Have you come across any cases of whooping cough yet?' Dr Dean brought her back to earth with a bang.

She shook her head, the gesture loosening yet another tendril of hair. She knew she looked a mess, navy uniform crumpled, hair untidy, shoes scuffed with all the walking, and she felt a stab of irritation with Dr Dean for keeping her from a warm bath and a change of clothing.

'I haven't seen any yet, but I've several children on my list for tomorrow,' she added.

'Margaret Gearing said there's one case over at Merton, but I've had none so far. I wish to God more mothers would have their babies immunised,' he went on sharply.

'I wish that, too, but with the very slight risk of——' Rosemary began, but he brushed her words aside.

'It's *your* duty, as a senior nurse, to overcome the qualms of these people. Margaret does her best, but health visitors don't wear a uniform, and parents take more notice of what a uniformed nurse says. Remember that!' he went on forcefully.

Rosemary was tempted to salute, but didn't think he was in the mood for silly jokes. The easygoing air was merely a camouflage, after all. Underneath, Dr Craig Dean was all steel!'

Irked by his attitude but trying hard not to show it, she saw him to the door. As he turned to make some comment, a short, rather skinny boy hailed him.

'Daddy Craig!' He flung himself at the tall doctor, and Rosemary turned her startled gaze on them both.

Dr Dean's lips tightened. 'Hello, Steve.' Gently he disentangled himself from the boy's grasp. 'This is Steven Abbott, Sister. Sister Miller is our new district nurse,' he explained.

Wide-spaced pale eyes surveyed Rosemary. Then the boy smiled, showing the gap in his front teeth. Encouraged by the doctor, he shook hands with her, then Rosemary was alone again.

She stayed in the doorway until man and small boy disappeared down the winding village street. Somewhere in the distance, church bells began to ring, and she let the sound wash over her, wishing the calm and beauty of the early evening could go on for ever.

So Lyn Abbott's son called the doctor 'Daddy', she mused as she turned reluctantly and closed the door. Mrs Abbott evidently intended to marry the doctor, and Rosemary wondered why she should mind so much. After all, *her* future lay with Alec Scott, or with no one. She and Alec belonged to each other, and she hoped her absence might cause him to miss her, just a little.

The next day dawned crisp and fresh, the sort of day that made Rosemary feel glad to be alive.

She was poring over her map of the district, wondering which patient on her list should come first, when she heard the postman. His tuneless early morning whistling was already familiar to her, but that was the first time he'd called.

She bit her lip savagely, drawing blood. Willing herself to finish her plan of campaign for the day, she hurried through it. First young Mrs Honeysett with her leg ulcer. The woman must be persuaded to see Dr Dean about it, whatever quarrels they might have had in the past. Then on to the Fairleys'? she wondered. No, surely the Council estate came before the farm? She bent her head to the map again, but it was no good; she could not concentrate until she'd picked up her letter.

Angry with herself for her weakness, she hurried to the front door. Most likely it was only a circular, or even a letter for the previous owner. It occurred to her that Alec didn't know her address, so it could hardly be from him.

She didn't know whether to be pleased or sorry that the envelope bore her Aunt Lizzie's handwriting. Of course she was glad to hear from her only aunt, but she really wished the letter had been from Alec. Just to see his bold black handwriting on the envelope, to know that he was missing her, that he was genuinely sorry for the little 'episodes'.

That was what he'd called them—episodes. Like chapters in a novel, she supposed, staring sightlessly into space for a moment. Romantic episodes. They meant nothing, he had assured her; forgotten by the following morning, he'd insisted. When she had pointed out that behaving like a stray tomcat did not endear him to her, they'd quarrelled. Not for the first time, of course. Usually after an argument, however fierce, they ended up in each other's arms, but not this time. Both of them said things that were better left unsaid, and not all Alec's loving persuasion had coaxed Rosemary into accepting his apologies. He'd had too many 'episodes' for her to forgive him yet again.

It was all over. She had returned his engagement ring despite his orders to her to keep it. Yes, *orders*! No man ordered *her* about! She'd been independent for too long. First Alec, now Craig Dean. Well, if *he* thought she would docilely accept his orders, he'd better think again!

As a GP, Dr Dean was the team-leader—that much she accepted. But she was a trained professional too, and if she felt a treatment ought to be changed, or that people like Mrs Cole should not take up the valuable time of a trained nurse, she would certainly say so.

She glared down at the envelope as if it was a combination of the two blue-eyed men, then smiled ruefully, her fingers automatically inching the envelope open as she returned to her list.

There was just time to wash up her breakfast things, then she must be away. She . . .

Her Aunt Lizzie's envelope was open, but Rosemary's eyes weren't on the letter. The loose pages fluttered unnoticed to the ground as she held up the small envelope which had been enclosed in the much larger one. A letter from Alec.

The envelope was sealed, and Rosemary turned it over and over, stroking it gently. It bore the inscription: 'For darling Rosemary', in Alec's big, firm writing.

For darling Rosemary. She repeated it to herself, then, feeling foolish, hurriedly slipped the envelope into her capacious shoulder-bag. She would save it for later. What he had to say might well make her angry. Even if it did not, she couldn't concentrate on it now. Duty called.

Hastily she gathered her aunt's letter together, then finished her list. She would read both letters at lunchtime. No doubt Aunt Lizzie would have some explanation for her.

It was a busy morning. Mr Krender, the terminal cancer patient, remained about the same, but Rosemary spent more time with him than was necessary. His elderly wife, too, needed support.

Supporting relatives was one of the tasks that might properly be delegated to the enrolled nurse or one of the auxiliaries, but Rosemary preferred to do that for herself. She had vast experience of caring for oncology patients and had spent some time as a voluntary worker in a hospice.

It was partly that period in her life that had led her towards community nursing. It was a challenge, and she preferred to work on her own, fitting her own routine and timetable around the patients. She had trained at one of the big teaching hospitals in London, then staffed there before taking the district nursing course.

She sighed a little. It was always sad reliving the past. Her mother had died when she was little, but her father had lived to see her finish her nursing training, had been proud to see her receive the hospital's gold medal for student of the year.

Would he be proud now? she wondered, as she made her way to the car after leaving the Krenders. Certainly he would not have taken to Alec Scott, who was worldly, successful, and yes, arrogant, too. Love for Alec did not blind her to his faults. Perhaps she loved him because of them. He was quite unlike any man she had met in the medical profession.

Dr Dean showed faint signs of arrogance, but perhaps their meetings would be few.

Still anxious to know what her ex-fiancé had to say, she nevertheless carried on with her visits.

'Young' Mrs Honeysett, as Gwen Sayers called her, looked drawn and ill when Rosemary at last found her in. It was her second call there, having received no reply to her first call earlier. Yet she was sure she had heard movement within the old cottage.

'Oh, it's you, Sister. Come on in,' Mrs Honeysett invited wanly. Her cottage had a tiny hall, but the sitting-room was dark and poky, and smelled of cats.

Mrs Honeysett shooed a large ginger cat off the chintz-covered settee so that Rosemary could sit down. Rosemary seated herself on the edge, and was glad she hadn't relaxed, for a pair of eyes glared balefully at her from behind one of the cushions.

Resisting the urge to jump up again, she began talking generally to put Mrs Honeysett at her ease. The subject of the ulcer and the very necessary visit to the surgery would need to be broached gradually.

After some minutes spent discussing the weather, Rosemary's former post, and community nursing, Mrs Honeysett stretched out her leg for Rosemary's inspection, peeling down a pair of laddered stockings.

'I don't cover it unless I go to the town,' she offered. 'It's best not covered, but it do stick so.'

Fortunately, the ulcer was only superficial as yet, but the woman needed to see Dr Dean. There might be an underlying cause, perhaps diabetes or a heart condition, and there was no way Rosemary could treat the ulcer without the man's permission.

When she told the patient this, there was a stunned silence for a moment. 'Oh dear me, no, I can't go back to him! Not after what I said about *her*!' she exclaimed at last.

Feeling that in this case firmness was needed, Rosemary emphasised the need for the doctor to take a quick look at the ulcer. 'After that, I can come to dress it for you. There are lots of treatments for leg ulcers now,' she coaxed. 'We'll soon have it healed.'

The woman looked doubtful. 'Well, I just don't know. I told him a few home truths and he didn't like it, Sister.' She eyed Rosemary defiantly.

'We none of us like home truths, but sometimes they clear the air, Mrs Honeysett. Doctor won't hold it against you, but he would be very angry if he could see your leg.'

'She's his lady-love, you see—that Lyn Abbott, I mean.' Mrs Honeysett leaned forward confidingly, and Rosemary wondered how she was to escape. She didn't want to hear gossip about Lyn Abbott; she had a feeling it would be unpalatable.

Fortunately, at that moment the ginger cat chose to regain his former seat, and Rosemary was glad to let him. The first and second cats bickered a little before settling down, and Mrs Honeysett smiled fondly at them, before reluctantly agreeing to think about attending surgery the next day.

Rosemary breathed deeply of the fresh air when

at length she emerged. She doubted that Mrs Honeysett *would* go to the doctors, and decided to convey her there herself, perhaps to the evening surgery.

Friday tomorrow, then the weekend free. Glancing at her watch, she saw that it was nearly one o'clock. Time to dash back to the cottage.

Her predecessor, Sister Pearson, had established a routine of returning to her home at lunchtime each day to receive calls. She had let it be known to GPs, the local hospital and the various emergency and voluntary services that she was available between one and two should anyone want to phone with a query. This seemed an excellent idea to Rosemary and one she had willingly adopted.

After checking her list for the afternoon, she turned the small car towards what she was coming to regard as 'home'. In the summer it would be very pleasant in the cottage. She could have Aunt Lizzie to stay and perhaps some of Aunt Lizzie's numerous friends——

Of course! Alec's letter! And she had almost forgotten it, *did* forget it completely during the morning's round. Poor Alec, he would be angry if he knew.

Eager to begin his letter, she remained in the car once back at the cottage. With the windows wound down she would hear the telephone clearly. With fingers that shook, she tore open the envelope and eagerly withdrew the two precious pages.

'Ah, I thought I'd catch you in!' Dr Craig Dean's face appeared at the car window, and Rosemary could have wept.

A supercilious smile hovered about his mouth as

he waited for her to regain control of her feelings. To have a visitor just at that moment! Particularly to have a visit from Craig Dean.

She forced a cool smile as she met his gaze. 'I try to get back lunchtimes, Doctor, in case I'm wanted.'

'I'm sure you're very much wanted, Sister Miller.'

The words were softly spoken and innocuous enough, but Craig Dean's sleepy blue eyes were sending a different message.

CHAPTER TWO

ROSEMARY felt obliged to invite the doctor into her cottage—after all, he could hardly be expected to discuss patients outside. In any case, she mused as she led the way indoors, she felt uncomfortable when he smiled down at her like that. His eyes were very blue and very innocent, angelic almost. But an angel he most certainly was not! The combination of innocence and sensuousness was alarming. At least with Alec one was never in any doubt as to his motive, but Craig Dean was in a class of his own.

Fortunately the telephone rang as she was inviting him to sit down. The caller was her health visitor colleague and Rosemary scribbled notes while they talked. She was so engrossed that she didn't notice the tall doctor disappear.

'There, that's that,' she said as she replaced the receiver, glancing round in surprise when she found she was alone.

Interesting sounds were coming from the kitchen, and she popped her head around the door.

Dr Dean was making himself at home with a vengeance! The salad roll she had intended for her lunch was on a large plate on the table, surrounded by the slices of cold chicken which were for her dinner. Her bemused gaze took in the extra salad vegetables and cole slaw, then Dr Dean glanced up.

'I've invited myself to lunch. Hope you don't mind,' he said amiably.

She distrusted him in this amiable mood, but murmured graciously that of course she didn't mind.

'Liar!' he chuckled, setting out the knives and forks. 'I bought some cole slaw and fresh ham at the general store, but I see you've already got some.'

'Yes,' said Rosemary weakly. Indeed, she couldn't think of anything else to say. He had so clearly intended lunching with her, and she wondered why.

'The ham I brought will do for your lunch tomorrow. I've put it in the fridge.'

She eyed him, a faint frown creasing her brow. He was being extremely kind and affable, and she wondered how long it would be before the fragile peace was broken. They ate in a companionable silence, Rosemary enjoying his company, despite her feeling of unease.

Alec's letter began to burn a hole in her pocket once they had finished the meal. When Dr Dean had appeared so abruptly, she had hurriedly stuffed the two letters in her uniform pocket. She had seen his eyes on Alec's letter, and he might have guessed its importance for her. Doctors didn't miss a thing!

Without realising it, she shot the doctor a sour look, then began to fidget with her knife.

'You're restless, Sister,' Dr Dean commented mildly.

'Restless? Am I? I—I suppose I was thinking of all the tasks I should be performing.' She summoned up a smile. 'Would you like a pudding? It's only ice cream, but there's plenty,' she offered.

'No, I won't eat any more now, thank you. I hope for a good dinner tonight.'

'Oh, yes. Naturally.' She supposed he was dining out with Lyn Abbott. She rose and automatically began gathering up the dishes; she could wash them later. It was high time she was on her way.

Thursday was, she knew, Dr Dean's half-day. It was half-day in the village too, with nearly all the shops being closed. A good afternoon to visit the working mothers on her list.

With a minor whooping cough epidemic beginning, the more mothers she could see, the better. Of course, primarily it was the health visitor's work, but Margaret needed help, if all the primary health care team chipped in with a little advice, the message would soon get across.

She put her hand in her pocket for her list, but her fingers touched the letter instead. Alec's letter. She couldn't go back to work, not knowing.

'Your restlessness is turning to agitation, Sister.' Craig Dean's quiet words brought her back to reality.

'I'm *not* agitated!' Her tone was sharper than she had intended. She was in the throes of probably unrequited love, and she didn't feel like a verbal sparring match with this man. 'I'm sorry, Doctor,' she murmured into the silence, 'I'm not myself today.'

If she expected sympathy or a reassuring smile, she was out of luck. His words were honest and brutal. 'I hope you aren't pining already for the man you've left behind!' His tone was sharp, and the colour left her face.

'You've no right to say that! I haven't left a man behind, anyway. I keep my private life *private*,' she emphasised, to let him know he was treading on dangerous ground.

'You must have a man hidden away somewhere,' he went on forcefully. 'It isn't likely a striking-looking woman like you is condemned to a lonely spinsterhood!'

Rosemary gasped at his effrontery. At the same time her brain registered the small compliment he had thrown her. 'I hope I won't be condemned to a lonely old age, Doctor,' she said, choosing her words carefully. 'However, I have a busy afternoon ahead of me, so . . .' She waited nervously.

Dr Dean moved nearer, and she was rooted to the spot for a moment, her eyes blazing defiance at him, as a smile tugged at the corners of his wide mouth.

Her lips parted involuntarily, but whether she intended to tell him to mind his own business, or whether it was a preliminary to being kissed, she would never know, for the telephone rang just then.

A small sigh escaped her as the tension left her body.

'Duty calls, Sister Miller,' Craig Dean said quietly. 'We must finish our . . . discussion another time.'

Without warning, he planted a kiss on the tip of her small snub nose, then strode out of the cottage.

Shaken and shattered, Rosemary reached for the telephone. Duty called, and she still didn't know what Alec wanted.

Eventually she found time to read the precious letter, though she chose to read her aunt's first. There would be explanations in that.

Aunt Lizzie always had a soft spot for Alec. His charm worked on women of all ages, and Aunt Lizzie was over sixty. The long lettter rambled on a bit, but at least fifty per cent of it concerned Alec. Aunt Lizzie finished by ordering her niece to overlook whatever minor faults Alec had.

Rosemary hesitated before opening the letter she had been longing for. It was mid-afternoon now, and she had only one more call to make. Deliberately she had made herself carry on with her work, as if tacitly accepting that Alec belonged in the past.

With fingers that trembled, she withdrew the two sheets of expensive white notepaper. The letter was warmer than she had expected, and also contained a wish to see her again. He ended with 'your ever-loving Alec.'

Ever-loving Alec. Was he? The cynicism he had bred in her would not evaporate, blow away in the wind. She so wanted to believe that he was truly sorry. Yet . . .'

Rosemary's last call was at Granny Cole's. She disliked addressing patients by such prefixes as 'Granny', 'Dad', and so on, but when she had enquired of a passer-by where she could find Mrs Primrose Cole, the woman at first said she didn't know anyone of that name. She knew a Granny Cole, though, and had given Rosemary complicated directions to the cottage.

It was more of a detached residence than a cottage, and Rosemary's own home would seem even smaller after this. It was set apart and was reached at the end of a short but potholed lane—a lane that would be a quagmire in winter, Rosemary thought in dismay. Surely the old woman didn't live alone? If she had a fall it would be hazardous for the ambulance to attempt the lane in bad weather, and valuable time would be lost.

Granny Cole did live alone, but she wasn't the little frail old dear Rosemary had imagined. True, she was small, less than five foot, but she didn't look frail or in need of sheltered accommodation, despite her eighty-seven years. She was a delightful, cheery little woman, and Rosemary enjoyed her visit more than she would have thought possible. Sister Pearson had apparently checked her blood pressure every now and again and taken blood samples. Granny wasn't actually ill but had hypertension. Dr Dean saw her at intervals of three months.

That information wasn't on Mrs Cole's medical record, though the doctor made the occasional note on it. If he saw her at regular intervals, they must have been house calls. Possibly she was a favourite of his, just as she'd been a favourite of Sister Pearson.

Rosemary could understand why this might be so. The old lady had a rich fund of stories about the village and its people. Then she casually asked Rosemary if she had met Lyn yet.

'Lyn? You mean Lyn Abbott? No, as a matter of fact, I haven't,' Rosemary admitted, hoping Mrs Cole wasn't going to tear Lyn's reputation to shreds. Lyn seemed to invoke strong reaction in people, and little of it was to her credit. If she hadn't been on a week's holiday, Rosemary would have met her by now and could have made up her own mind. She disliked prejudging people, but with Lyn Abbott it would be hard not to.

'Lyn is my granddaughter.' Mrs Cole sprang her surprise and sat back to watch Rosemary's face.

It certainly *was* a surprise. It was a wonder that Gwen Sayers hadn't mentioned it. 'I didn't realise she was a relative,' Rosemary said carefully. 'At least she must be a comfort to you. Being a trained nurse, she——'

'Comfort! Her?' Mrs Cole actually snorted. 'I never see her. She don't come near her old granny, not her!'

The old woman folded her arms and glared at Rosemary.

Fearful for Mrs Cole's high blood pressure, Rosemary attempted to undo the harm she had unwittingly caused. 'I'm sorry, but I'm a stranger and couldn't be expected to know you were estranged from Mrs Abbott. Please forgive me.' She smiled tentatively, and Mrs Cole cackled.

'It's all right, you wasn't to know. Doctor visits instead—the young doctor,' she explained, and Rosemary nodded, her face expressionless.

Once she had seen that Mrs Cole wanted for nothing and was apparently happy, she prepared to leave, but not before a paper bag full of home-made scones had been pressed into her hands.

Rosemary was on the doorstep before Mrs Cole delivered her parting shot. 'I've got the sight, you know.'

'Oh?' Rosemary was startled but did not show it. A lot of country people believed they had second sight, and it wasn't her place to tell the woman there was no such thing. It was uncanny what these rural old folk knew.

'Yes. Second sight, you'd call it,' Mrs Cole went on. 'My mother had it and her mother before her. My mother used to point the finger at people who upset her, and sure enough, summat terrible would happen to them,' she said with relish.

'I don't think that's second sight, Mrs Cole,' Rosemary said firmly. 'It's a kind of superstition. Something to do with witchcraft in the old days, I believe.'

'My Lyn's like that. Don't you go taking anything she wants for herself, Sister. Well, see you another time.' Mrs Cole shut the door abruptly, leaving Rosemary considerably disquieted.

Lyn is like that. Like what? Surely an educated young woman would not believe in stupid superstitions? Of course the whole thing was ridiculous, but it made Rosemary long to meet this Lyn Abbott, with or without her broomstick!

Their meeting was sooner than she expected, for Lyn was in Dr Dean's surgery the following morning when Rosemary arrived for the weekly meeting of the primary care team.

This took place mid-morning after surgery. Rosemary was able to meet one of the nursing auxiliaries who had been off duty. The remainder of the team consisted of the health visitor, Margaret Gearing, the district SEN who was directly responsible to Rosemary herself, and several auxiliaries. These latter, all part-time, did the more mundane chores such as bed-bathing, assisting patients in the bathroom, shaving and so on.

The two doctors completed the team, plus Lyn Abbott, who attended in her capacity as an SRN. She used to run the minor ailment clinic as well as acting as evening receptionist, and helped out wherever she could. This information came from the State Enrolled Nurse, Mrs Partridge, and was almost the first good thing Rosemary had heard about her. It counterbalanced the 'malevolent witch' image, anyway! No doubt Mrs Cole was biased, due to some family quarrel, perhaps.

The group began to get restless when Dr Dean was a long time joining them, being still closeted with Lyn. Dr Tunstall was out on an urgent visit and might not be back before the meeting broke up. They all had work to get on with, and Rosemary would have buzzed Dr Dean if it had been anyone else in his room. She had no right to interfere in his private life, but she began to resent Lyn Abbott for taking up his valuable time, probably for no good reason.

When at length they appeared, Dr Dean was grim-faced, and Lyn's small, heart-shaped face bore signs of tears.

Despite Granny Cole's words, Rosemary could find no trace of the evil-minded creature she had half pictured. Lyn Abbott was tall and slender, with brunette hair cut short in a gamin style that Rosemary thought suited her particularly well. Although not technically beautiful, her features were small and regular, her eyes an unusual shade of tawny-yellow. Cats' eyes, Rosemary thought, as Dr Dean introduced them.

Lyn's smile was cool, her handshake even cooler, but she sat beside Rosemary and seemed disposed to be courteous and helpful, if not actually friendly. On first acquaintance Rosemary could expect no more.

Craig Dean eyed them covertly as he sipped his now cold coffee. Rosemary glanced up from her notes and caught him watching them. District nursing Sister and GP exchanged glances, Rosemary raising one brow slightly. That crooked smile she had come to know crossed his face, then the meeting began.

It was as they were all trooping out later that it happened. Young Steve Abbott appeared from nowhere, or so it seemed. He was on his cycle pedalling furiously down the hill which led to the surgery. There was a zig-zag bend in the road when it passed the surgery, and cars coming from the opposite direction were temporarily unsighted.

The accident was partly Lyn's fault. She screamed out to her son to be careful. He couldn't have heard her, but he saw her wave, and this momentarily distracted his attention. The driver of the car coming from the opposite direction had no chance of avoiding the boy, though he swung his wheel hard over.

Steve was hit a glancing blow and knocked from his cycle. Dr Dean headed the group who ran up to the boy lying so still by the side of the road.

Seeing that Lyn and Dr Dean were with the boy, Rosemary stopped to reassure the driver, who was white with shock. After she had tended him, she hurried up to the others. Mrs Partridge passed her, heading for the surgery, muttering 'Ambulance' as she passed.

Steve was, she saw, alive and not apparently hurt.

'Nothing fractured that I can tell,' Dr Dean said tersely. 'A few cuts and bruises, and he's shocked.'

Lyn was sobbing loudly, and Rosemary went to put a comforting arm around her shoulder, but the woman shrugged her away, clutching at Dr Dean's arm instead as he attempted to carry out a full examination of the boy.

He murmured soothing words, and gradually Lyn's sobs stopped. Rosemary felt for her, but couldn't see that breaking down in the street did anyone any good. Steve was staring up at his mother, then he began to cry as well. Rosemary knelt by his side and took his small hand in hers, just as the ambulance arrived, the ambulance station being close by.

She offered to accompany the boy to the local hospital, but his mother curtly refused. 'He's my son! Do you think I can't cope?' she snapped.

'Lyn, stop that!' Dr Dean took her firmly by the arm. 'Sister was only trying to help.'

'Everyone calls it "trying to help", but I think it's interference!' The tears began to roll down Lyn's cheeks again and Rosemary felt desperately sorry for her. She was clearly a sick woman, perhaps depressed by the impending divorce. It could be that there was some wrangling over the custody of the child, then on top of that there was the shock of his accident. No wonder something had snapped!

Rosemary's eyes met Craig Dean's and there was a moment of understanding between them. Whatever his personal feelings for Lyn, his professional interest in her came first, and they must both strive to set her on the path to good health again.

This time Lyn did not shrug off Rosemary's comforting arm and Rosemary led her away, leaving the doctor to follow the ambulance in his car.

Lyn could pack a few necessities for Steve, and Rosemary intended to drive her to the hospital as soon as possible.

'Look after her, Sister,' Dr Dean said softly. His tender smile was for Lyn alone, though, and Rosemary wished desperately that she had someone to smile at her like that.

CHAPTER THREE

THE REST of the day passed in such a whirl of activity that Rosemary nearly forgot Mrs Honeysett. She was just leaving her last patient when she remembered—she had to persuade Mrs Honeysett to accompany her to evening surgery.

Fortunately the doctors didn't have an appointment system, so it was simply a matter of turning up and sitting in the waiting-room. If there was too long a wait, Mrs Honeysett would probably disappear, so Rosemary needed to be there too.

Steve Abbott had been extremely lucky, and had suffered only cuts and a nasty bruise on his buttocks. The hospital was keeping him in overnight, but he was in much better shape than his mother. Lyn seemed to have gone to pieces, and was spending the night with the Tunstalls.

Dr Tunstall and his wife lived in the house which was also used as the surgery. Rosemary didn't know where Dr Dean lived. Idly she speculated on it as she turned her car in the direction of Mrs Honeysett's cottage. There were several houses of character en route, and she picked a special one for Craig Dean.

She had passed it several times already but never seen any sign of life. It was set back from the road, the front garden being mainly paved. She could only guess at the sort of garden there would be behind the house. Gardens in this area tended to be

large, and she judged that this house might have
half an acre or so. There would have to be plenty of
trees and some small ground-covering plants so
that he needn't spend much effort on it. She would
have planted a flowering cherry in the front, but of
course the concrete courtyard was more serviceable.

Rosemary decided that the house probably had
four bedrooms and a big sitting-room. It had
friendly mullioned windows and an air of welcome
that she found irresistible. She wished she could
afford such a house herself.

Mrs Honeysett did not need much persuasion
after all, though Rosemary knew the woman
wouldn't have bothered if she had had to make her
own way to the surgery.

Afterwards, she offered to run the woman home,
but she intended visiting a friend while she was in
the village. Dr Dean came out as Rosemary was
rummaging in her bag to see if she had enough
money on her. The fast food business hadn't quite
reached Hurstfield, but in the neighbouring market
town there was a Chinese takeaway. It would save
cooking, for she was exhausted after her first week.
A nice cosy takeaway meal by the fire was exactly
what she needed. She would bath first, then wrap
herself in the pretty dressing-gown Aunt Lizzie had
given her for her twenty-sixth birthday the previous
month.

But her unexciting plans were nearly changed,
for when she glanced up, Craig Dean was watching
her. His lean, athletic body was framed by the
doorway, and those sleepy eyes were half closed.

She wondered if he knew the effect he had on

women. Probably, she reflected, as she said crisply: 'I'll be off now, doctor. I hope you have a quiet weekend.'

'Have dinner with me.'

It was a statement, and she paused, taken aback. 'Dinner? With you?' She knew it was a stupid rejoinder, but she couldn't think straight for a moment.

'Why not with me? I don't bite!' he chuckled. 'I'll pick you up about eight. I can't come before, I've a couple of visits.'

He turned back to his surgery before Rosemary could recover her scattered wits. Delight flooded through her. An evening out was just what she needed to prevent her from thinking about Alec. Then she remembered someone else.

Frowning, she poked her head around the door. Dr Dean turned, windcheater slung casually over one shoulder.

He was an extremely attractive man, even in casual clothes, and Rosemary's eyes darkened with pain. 'You can't take me to dinner,' she pointed out reluctantly. 'What about Lyn?'

'Oh, good God! I'd forgotten Lyn,' he admitted, with a rueful smile.

'Forgotten?' she echoed. 'How can you forget the woman you're going to ma——' Hastily she tried to change the sentence, but it was too late.

He moved closer, close enough for her to smell his rather nice aftershave. 'Yes, Sister? You were saying?' Gone was the sensuous smile. A muscle jerked at the corner of his mouth, and she was irresistibly reminded of Alec in a temper.

Having started, she might as well burn her boats

completely. 'If you encourage the little boy to call
you Daddy then it seems reasonable to assume that
you're going to marry his mother,' Rosemary said
coldly. He needn't think he could take out his
temper on *her*!

She knew she was glaring at him, knew also that
she was being very foolish, but she could not help
herself. He brought out the worst in her already,
and this was only their first week of working
together!

'*You* might assume that I'm going to marry Lyn,'
he said after a moment. 'No one else does. Lyn's
divorce isn't through. She's still a married woman.
Remember that, Sister Miller.' There was an edge
to his voice, but rashly Rosemary ignored it.

'Then you shouldn't let Steve call you his daddy!
It isn't fair to the poor little c——'

She wasn't allowed to finish, for the tall doctor
moved with a speed that surprised her. He had a
lazy, almost indolent way of walking and smiling,
but it was clearly an act to disarm people.

She nibbled her full lower lip in dismay as he
stared down at her, a thoughtful expression on his
face. He made no move to touch her, yet she felt as
though he had. There was something tangible in the
air, and he seemed to feel it, too. She held her
breath, all thoughts of Lyn, Steve, and Chinese
takeaways vanishing as if they had never been.

Blue eyes met grey ones, and there was a long
moment of silence—a painful silence for Rosemary, for she found she could not lower her glance,
could not break the power Craig Dean held over
her at that moment.

Then that lazy smile broke out again. 'I do *not*

encourage Steve to call me Daddy Craig. It's a habit he's picked up,' he said quietly, and Rosemary found herself nodding understandingly. 'If it gives him a feeling of security, I have no right to object,' he went on slowly. 'I feel sorry for the poor little chap.'

'So do I,' Rosemary admitted. 'His mother is far from well, and I can quite see that you can't hurt the boy's feelings or hers.'

'Lyn had a bad time with her husband. Now he's threatening to take Steve away from her. She's going through hell at the moment, so be kind to her.' He turned away abruptly, and Rosemary hurriedly picked up her bag and left.

Blackberries were still everywhere in evidence, and she picked one from the cane that grew by Dr Tunstall's front gate. She gazed down at it absently. Poor Lyn and poor Steve. There was always someone worse off, she reflected sadly, as she drove home.

Although Dr Dean's first duty was to Lyn, it *would* have been pleasant to dine with him. Of course, he would want to talk shop. Indeed, there would be no point in asking her out otherwise.

She decided against the Chinese meal, after all; for some reason she had lost her appetite. After her bath, she made herself some scrambled egg and took the tray into the sitting-room. Aunt Lizzie's gift was a trifle tight and Rosemary knew she must lose weight, but the colour suited her admirably. The deep, rich blue lent warmth to her pale complexion, and the expensive velvet of the dressing-gown made her feel like a rich lady of leisure.

She decided she would reply to Aunt Lizzie's

letter after her meal. The one from Alec had a question mark hanging over it. Although she wanted to see him again, Craig Dean had already told her he hoped she wasn't pining for the man she'd left behind. He would view Alec Sott's arrival in the village without enthusiasm.

The scrambled egg finished, she left the dishes to soak, then padded barefoot back to the fire. Stretching her long, shapely legs out in front of her, she sprawled inelegantly in the armchair and closed her eyes. It was then that the doorbell rang, and she tensed.

Surely it wasn't a patient? Everyone on the list knew where she lived, so it could well be. It was past eight now and dark outside, and she was reluctant to answer the bell, which rang imperiously several times more.

Alec! Rosemary glanced in dismay at her dressing-gown. She couldn't see him like this! He would be quick to take advantage of her unpreparedness. Before she knew it, he would be kissing her, and then who could say where it would end?

Fortunately she had had a chain fitted on the door, a habit she had acquired when living in the city, so if it *was* Alec, she could keep him out.

It was Craig Dean she found on the doorstep as she opened the door as far as the chain would permit.

'Oh, Dr Dean! Can I help you?' she murmured, taken aback.

His amused glance took in the situation. 'Did I disturb you in the bath? I'm afraid I'm a bit late.'

'Late for what?' she asked through the chink.

'I feel slightly ridiculous standing here like a

salesman,' he said mildly, and she flushed.

'Yes I—I'm sorry, I didn't think.' Feeling foolish, she opened the door and invited him inside.

'It's a habit I got into. The chain on the door, I mean,' she explained, flustered at the doctor catching her in dressing-gown and bare feet, and literally with her hair down. She let it out of its neat bun once she was off duty, and the naturally wavy flaxen hair hung almost to her waist. It made her look young and vulnerable—she knew that because Alec had told her so, many times. Natural blondes fascinated him. All his girl-friends were fair, those she knew of, anyway. It seemed odd that Alec liked only blondes and Craig Dean opted only for brunettes!

She didn't recall asking Craig to sit down, but he did so, leaning back on the small settee, arms folded comfortably behind his head.

'Will you be long' he asked, as he relaxed against the cushions. 'I booked the table for half-past.'

Stupefied, Rosemary could only stare. 'You mean dinner?' When he nodded, she went on: 'But what about Lyn? You were going to spend the evening with her!'

'*You* might have thought so,' he agreed calmly. 'I popped up to see her and she's perfectly happy with my aunt fussing over her. I went to the General to see Steve as well, but he was fast asleep. So, having performed my chores, I can now go out and enjoy myself. Hurry up, there's a good girl,' he added, when she stood still rooted to the spot.

'Yes, Doctor,' she said, so meekly that his laughter followed her up the stairs.

Feeling like a teenager again, she dressed hastily,

wishing she had time for a full make-up. She wore
little make-up on duty, and it ought to be creamed
off and a fresh layer applied. Then there was that
new shade of lipstick one of her former colleagues
had insisted she try.

In the end, she had to settle for a trace of the new
lipstick and a quick dab with a powderpuff.

There was no suitable restaurant in the village, so
they drove to what Craig described as his favourite
restaurant in Haywards Heath. It was fairly new
and Rosemary had never dined there before. Aunt
Lizzie *would* be surprised if she could see her now!

Rosemary wondered how she would view Craig.
Her aunt was such a fan of Alec that she might not
take to the tall, craggy doctor. She wasn't aware
that she was staring, until he commented on it. She
gave what she hoped was a merry laugh as she
apologised.

'I was miles away! Sorry and all that.' Quickly
she busied herself with the enormous menu-card.

'How many miles away, I wonder?' His tone was
thoughtful, and she glanced up sharply.

'My aunt lives just outside the town and I was
wondering what she would think of you,' she said
candidly.

'And what do *you* think of me?' he countered.

She lowered her gaze and pretended to consult
the menu. 'I haven't made up my mind yet, Doctor,'
she told him, and he chuckled.

'I'm easygoing if handled right,' he assured her.
'The chicken here is superb. They have a secret
recipe for the sauce, I believe.'

Meekly Rosemary agreed to have the chicken,
after a melon starter.

They talked little until they were well under way with the main course, then Craig began to question her about her work in the tough inner-city areas.

Surprised and pleased, Rosemary plunged into a detailed account of a project she had started there and which was continuing. 'There isn't enough done about preventing illness,' she stressed as she finished. 'In a depressed environment like that, the sick outnumber the healthy.'

He nodded slowly. 'I would like to start a "well person" clinic here. I worked in Birmingham during my early GP years, so I know what a challenge that type of environment is. Hurstfield is a refreshing change—at least for a while.'

Rosemary felt a stab of disappointment. 'Are you expecting to leave, then? I thought you were settled here. With Dr Tunstall, I mean,' she faltered on, arrested by something in his glance.

'Settled. Oh, dear, that makes me sound like some doddery old biddy,' Craig Dean said slowly, blue eyes on her face. 'Do you honestly think I intend to spend the rest of my career buried away here? My uncle might be settled for life, but not me!'

He spoke forcefully, and Rosemary wondered at the chains which bound him to the village.

'Will you go to Africa, do you think' she asked with real interest, allowing her wine-glass to be topped up again.

Working in Africa was an idea that had often occurred to her. A lot of her patients had been of African origin, and she had once toyed with the idea of offering her services to Voluntary Service Overseas, to see the immigrant peoples in their natural setting. It would be a chance to tackle their problems on their home territory, and she wondered if Craig felt the same.

'I have a friend working in the Sudan. We trained together, and he's gone out there for two years to set up a clinic. I'm tempted,' he admitted.

She hadn't particularly thought about working in the Sudan, but certainly there must be a crying need for nurses there, and in Ethiopia, another famine-stricken country. Some of the television pictures had been heartbreaking.

'What about Lyn?' she couln't help asking, and Craig glanced at her sharply. 'She needs all the support she can get,' she added, and he agreed curtly that she did.

He made no further mention of Africa, and it was clear that Lyn Abbott was the stumbling block. He felt responsible for the woman, whether he loved her or not. She was a burden he would not shed, and Rosemary admired him for it.

After she mentioned Lyn, he clammed up, and, desperate for a safe topic of conversation, she began to speak of an article she had read in *The Lancet*, which concerned the particular needs of Afro-Caribbean communities.

'Knowledgeable as well as pretty!' he commented, and she flushed with pleasure.

'Thank you, kind sir!' she laughed. Perhaps she had drunk too much wine, for there were tears mingled with the laughter, and she hastily dabbed at her face with the table-napkin.

'Poor Rosemary! Are you so unhappy?' He leaned nearer, neatly plucking the napkin from her nerveless fingers.

She tried to laugh again, but couldn't make it. 'I'm sorry, I think I'm a bit drunk,' she admitted candidly, and he smiled lazily at her.

She rather wished he wouldn't smile at her like that. In her present dazed state she found the smile devastating. Those sleepy, heavy lidded eyes were half closed, and she swallowed nervously.

'I've had an exhausting week. Do you think we might go now?' she begged, wishing she could be alone to have a good cry. Why, she didn't know. It must have been too much wine, coupled with her heartache over Alec.

One strong hand closed over hers in a gesture of understanding, and she smiled gratefully through the mist of unshed tears. Craig's grip tightened briefly, then he turned aside to settle the bill, allowing her time to compose herself.

He was being immensely kind, much more so than she deserved. She had behaved foolishly, letting this man see the tender inner core that she kept hidden behind the cool, workaday district nurse image. She felt exposed, naked even.

It was a little before eleven when they arrived back at her cottage, and Rosemary turned to him gratefully, thanking him for the meal and his under-standing.

If she had hoped he would leave her, she was to be disappointed, for he insisted on seeing her in-doors, even switching on all the lights in the cottage while she plugged in the kettle.

Presumably he would want coffee, she thought wearily, as he went upstairs to see that everything was all right. She felt obliged to offer since she had deprived him of coffee at the restaurant. Her head ached just a little, and she felt as though her feet hardly touched the ground as she moved from kitchen to sitting-room and settled herself on the settee.

The log-effect fire gave out just enough heat for her, and she kicked off the uncomfortable sandals and closed her eyes. She intended slipping out of her best dress and undoing her bra once she was alone.

Half opening her eyes, she glanced thoughtfully down at the pretty silky dress, wondering if navy blue was quite right for blondes. Wondering, too, what Alec was doing at that moment.

A tear forced its way through her lashes, and, half asleep, she reached for her hankie. Then it was prised from her grasp, and Craig Dean gently wiped away the few tears that fell.

'Silly of me,' murmured Rosemary, curiously soothed by his strong presence.

'Very silly,' Craig agreed quietly. 'He isn't worth your tears, Rosemary. No man is.'

He stood back, while she scrambled to her feet. She was annoyed, and resentful of his remark. How could he know what Alec was like? He had no right to pre-judge him.

In full control of herself now, she gave what she hoped was a bright smile, then began to thank Craig anew for the evening out. After all, she had enjoyed most of the evening.

Curtly, he brushed aside her words. 'I'm sorry your memories are so painful, Rosemary. Perhaps you should try living in the present, instead of the past!' he finished brutally.

'You can't possibly know what——' she began,

but the words died away, as his lips met hers.

It was a savage onslaught, rather than a mere kiss, and they were both shaken as they drew apart. 'That will keep you going until your ex-lover turns up!' Craig snapped.

Speechless, Rosemary could only watch as he slammed out of the cottage. She felt as if he had slapped her. How could he be so unfeeling, so cruel?

His heartless attitude strengthened her resolve to invite Alec down. Let the arrogant doctor make of it what he would—*his* opinion was of no interest to her. He had Lyn Abbott.

Monday was hectic, and Rosemary threw herself into her work with renewed enthusiasm. Alec was coming to see her during the week.

After much soul-searching, she had phoned him on Saturday morning, and the sound of his voice brought tears to her eyes. Everything, she knew, would be all right once they were together again. She had suggested he stay with Aunt Lizzie after all, and he had agreed, surprisingly meek for once.

It was better that he stayed at Haywards Heath. There was always the possibility that Dr Dean might call in at the cottage, and she did not want the two men to meet if it could be avoided. The doctor, with his sharp-honed tongue and caustic wit, would wound poor Alec deeply.

Monday brought Rosemary's first case of whooping cough. His mother was one of Dr Tunstall's patients, and the old doctor called to see Rosemary at lunchtime.

As luck would have it, she had placed Alec's

photograph on the kitchen table while she ate a
hurried salad. It was the first time she had brought
it out since arriving in the village, though she kept it
in her bedside drawer, and glanced at it every night
before bed.

Deep blue eyes smiled at her from the ornate gilt
frame, and she was smiling foolishly back at the
photograph when Dr Tunstall thumped at the door.
Hastily she placed Alec face downwards before
opening the door.

'Only me!' rumbled Dr Tunstall, stepping inside
without waiting for an invitation. To her dismay, he
made straight for the kitchen.

'Ah, I thought I smelled tea! Where do you keep
the cups?'

Smiling despite her fear that he would see Alec's
picture, Rosemary settled him firmly into a chair,
then brought out a mug for his tea.

'I've got some biscuits,' she offered. 'Or there's
cherry madeira cake—homemade.'

'Tempting hussy! I can't resist homemade cake.
Did I tell you I do a bit of baking?'

Surprised, she shook her head, and the doctor's
eyes strayed to a wisp of hair that shook itself free.

'Strange—you being blonde, I mean. I suppose
Gwen has told you that "Doctor never does chase
blondes"?'

'I—I beg your pardon?' She coloured faintly,
because that was exactly what Gwen Sayers had
told her!

'Craig. He doesn't go for blondes. Likes 'em
dark and exotic-looking. Thin as rakes, most of his
girl-friends,' the doctor grumbled as he cut himself
a generous slice of cherry cake.

'I believe there are lots of things Doctor never does,' Rosemary said calmly. 'It's one of Gwen's favourite expressions!'

He nodded, his mouth full. Unlike his nephew, he had dark, piercing eyes, and they surveyed her dispassionately.

'You'd be good for young Craig—take him out of himself a bit. He's too tense.'

'Is he? He's never struck me that way.'

'Oh? Been taking an interest in him, have you?' He raised a bushy grey brow, and Rosemary shook her fist at him.

'Fiend! Stop fishing and tell me what you want. Is this purely a social visit?'

'This is my lunch. Got too many visits to go home for a proper break,' he explained. 'Had a case of whooping cough in the surgery this morning. Have you seen any yet?'

'Not here, no. The experts predict an epidemic, I know. Margaret Gearing has seen one or two already.'

'Mothers must be encouraged to have their babies immunised. It's the only way, Sister.'

'Please call me Rosemary. I notice that your nephew does now, even though I didn't invite him to,' she added tartly, and the old doctor guffawed.

'He's like that—never waits to be asked. Can't think who he takes after!' he added, with a twinkle.

'About the immunisation, Doctor,' she began. 'I always put in a word whenever I visit families with children, but there *are* slight risks attached—you can't deny that.'

Grudgingly he admitted the truth of that. 'Would

you have your baby protected against it?' he challenged, and Rosemary nodded emphatically.

'Most certainly I would. I once saw a child die of whooping cough, and I haven't forgotten that.'

While she was talking, Dr Tunstall absently picked up the photograph of Alec, and Rosemary tensed as he studied it carefully.

'This the man you love?' Shrewd dark eyes bored into hers, and she agreed reluctantly that it was.

'His name is Alec Scott. I—I knew him in the Midlands. We quarrelled and . . .' She broke off, getting up abruptly to clear away the dishes.

'So you ran away,' the balding doctor finished for her, and she whirled around.

'No, I did nothing of the sort! I wanted a change and . . . Yes, perhaps I did,' she admitted reluctantly. 'I'd had enough of big city work, so the quarrel with Alec did me a favour. Here I am in Ashdown Forest, breathing lovely clean country air. I needed a break from everything.'

He nodded. 'He's a handsome fellow. I expect he's arrogant and conceited with it. I know Craig is!' he chuckled, patting her on the shoulder before striding out, leaving a bewildered Rosemary to finish clearing the table.

She didn't know why she'd told him all that about Alec. Yet he had seemed to understand. He was rather a pet, beneath the gruff exterior.

Alec's photo was safely stowed away in her dressing-table drawer before she set out on her afternoon visits. Craig Dean must never be allowed to see the photo, or meet Alec. She was determined on that. She trusted Dr Tunstall and felt that he would not gossip about her love life. It was highly unlikely his nephew would be interested, anyway. That thought should have given her comfort, but for some reason it did not. In fact, it rankled.

She included the whooping cough family in her visits, although there was little she could do. There were no dressings to change, no appliances to be fitted. Yet she could give counsel, let the mother cry on her shoulder, if need be.

The child was just over a year old, and hadn't been immunised. 'We couldn't take the risk, Sister,' his mother said defensively. 'There's all this talk about brain damage.'

Rosemary could have painted a lurid picture of the extensive damage caused by the whooping cough itself, but that would have been cruel—and unnecessary. The parents, a very young couple, would see the outcome for themselves. A cough could go on for anything up to twelve weeks, and with a tiny child that could be nearly half its lifetime. After the coughing bout, the baby often ended up vomiting, and became more and more debilitated.

'Parents seem to think whooping cough is a relatively minor illness,' Rosemary said gently, 'but it isn't. It can kill.'

'Troy won't die, will he?' His mother raised her tear-stained face in alarm.

'Doctor says it's a mild dose, but I'll ask Miss Gearing, the health visitor, to call to see you. She's got some helpful booklets, and she knows far more about the disease than I do.'

It was true. Margaret Gearing had been funded

to do some research into the side-effects of whooping cough, and she was the best person to advise. She held twice-montly health education classes for parents and parents-to-be, and never failed to reinforce the message—immunise your child! The risk of brain damage could not be ignored, but the risk was extremely slight, and far less than the evil after-effects of the whooping cough itself. These could include fits, hernia, pneumonia and even collapsed lungs, yet still parents hesitated.

Margaret couldn't see why they didn't all queue up for the three injections, but Rosemary took a more practical view. If there was even a one-in-a-million chance of brain damage, caring parents would want to consider the matter carefully. Thank goodness the Princess of Wales had led the way by having her children immunised. It all helped, she reflected, as she drove home.

She found an unexpected visitor waiting outside her cottage. Two, in fact. Steve Abbott sat dejectedly on the doorstep, firmly clutching a piece of string to which was attached a large and exceedingly ugly dog.

Rosemary shooed them both inside as soon as she had unlocked the door, and the pair followed her into the warmth of the kitchen.

The dog was bigger than the boy and looked like a stray. His grizzled grey coat was threadbare, and Rosemary could see the outline of his ribs. Big brown eyes were fixed on her in mute appeal, and she thought of the minute steak she had intended as a treat for her dinner.

With a wry smile, she fetched it. He was probably used to raw food, when he was fed at all, but she flash-fried the steak, wishing she had something more substantial for him. He could probably eat a dozen such steaks and still be hungry!

The dog evidently thought the steak was a starter, for it disappeared in two gulps and he looked up for more. Rosemary shook her head. 'That's it, I'm afraid. All gone,' she added with an expressive gesture, and the hound lay down beside the boy, eyes still fixed hopefully on her.

'He's called Spike,' offered Steve. 'That's what I've called him, anyway. My best friend at school's called Spike 'cos he doesn't like being called Sidney.'

Rosemary chuckled. 'No, I imagine he doesn't. Have you had the dog long?'

He shuffled uncomfortably. 'Only just now. I found him, really I did!' Earnest eyes gazed at her.

'And you took him home, did you?' she prompted.

He nodded. 'I took him to the door, but Mum wouldn't let him in. She said he's got fleas.'

'I expect he has. We ought to get in touch with the police and the RSPCA. They'll take him in until his owner is found. He must belong to someone, Steve,' Rosemary added gently. The boy was near to tears, as he hugged the dog defensively.

He had quite recovered from his accident, but Lyn still had the worry of his father demanding custody. Although the stray was Lyn's problem, Rosemary began to feel as though she had taken over all the woman's problems, all her heartache. Probably Craig Dean felt the same way.

Some people had the facility for unloading their difficulties on to others, making other people feel

so sorry for them that they ended up with most
of the burdens! Lyn Abbott was clearly such a
person.

CHAPTER FOUR

STEVE was speaking again, and Rosemary dragged her mind back to the immediate difficulty—what to do with one flea-bitten stray dog.

'He doesn't belong to anybody, honestly, Sister,' the boy said earnestly. He plucked at Rosemary's sleeve and she felt as though he was plucking at her heartstrings as well. 'I *found* him,' he added.

Spike, it transpired, was tied to a tree in a remote part of the Forest. Ashdown Forest itself was partly shrubland now, but in places its former glory remained, and Steve had been exploring on his own when he had heard a dog whining and howling.

'He's got nobody, Sister, only me.' Boy and dog eyed her reproachfully, as if daring to suggest they should be parted.

Although she was an animal lover, the idea of Spike sharing her home did not appeal over-much. A smile broke out as she visualised Alec's reaction to a large, hairy dog!

'We'll have to tell the police—just in case he's been reported missing,' she warned. 'Someone may have stolen Spike and tied him to the tree as a nasty joke.' It wasn't likely, of course. He was hardly the sort of dog who would allow himself to be taken away.

Not the sort of dog one really wanted in a clean, tidy house either, come to that, Rosemary mused once she had seen Steve safely home. He had been overjoyed at her offer to look after Spike, but he was the only one who was pleased.

Neither Rosemary nor the dog enjoyed the medicated bath, and he strenuously objected to being dried. Instead, he shook himself all over her, soaking the kitchen as well as her. It had seemed easier to bath him in an old zinc bath indoors; that way he couldn't escape. Unfortunately, although he got in willingly, the bath wasn't big enough, and Rosemary had great difficulty in manoeuvring his body around so that she could wash him.

It was just as well that he wasn't a vicious dog, she reflected wryly, as she tried to dry him with her best bath towel, the only towel with a deep enough pile to absorb the water.

They were struggling together when the front doorbell rang. Thankfully, Rosemary got to her feet. She didn't want company, but an emergency would be preferable to dog wrestling!

Face flushed, hair awry, and dressed in scruffy jeans and sweater, she inched the door open, glad of Spike's protection if not of his company. He had emitted a deep-throated howl when the bell rang, and might have frightened the caller away.

But the caller was still there, and Alec Scott's laughing eyes met Rosemary's astonished gaze.

'Alec!' Hastily she unchained the door, then she was in his arms, her carefully-laid plan of being cool and unforgiving totally forgotten as she gave herself up to the ecstasy of his kiss.

Unfortunately, Spike did not share her enthusiasm, for he growled as Rosemary invited Alec in. Man and dog eyed each other, and Rosemary began to see the drawbacks of having a watchdog in the house.

She tried to coax Spike to be friends with Alec, but to no avail. 'I'll shut him in the kitchen,' she offered. 'I'll have to finish drying him first, though. He'll catch a chill.' She shepherded the reluctant dog out to the kitchen, and this time managed to dry most of him.

Alec was relaxing against the settee cushions when Rosemary emerged, but in her mind she saw Craig Dean sprawled there instead. Yet physically the two men were totally unlike, except for being tall. Alec was broader in the shoulder, barrel-chested, darker complexioned.

He smiled up at her, perfect white teeth gleaming in the tanned face. 'Did you miss me, Rosemary?' he asked softly, and she gave a rueful smile.

Denial was useless. Hadn't she thrown herself into his arms the moment he appeared? 'I may have done. I really can't remember,' she prevaricated, and Alec laughed, that throaty laugh she had once found so irresistible.

She joined in, but even their joint laughter couldn't drown out the whines from Spike, now securely shut in the kitchen, and she had to let him out.

Giving in to him would be bad if she intended training him to be obedient, but she still hoped another owner could be found for him. She intended asking Lyn if she would reconsider her decision. The dog would, at least, be company for the woman, and Steve would be overjoyed.

Alec and Rosemary ate supper in silence. Rosemary thought longingly of the steak Spike had eaten, but cheered herself with the thought that his need had been urgent. Now, of course, he was hungry again. She would have to buy him a case of dog food first thing in the morning.

It was as they were finishing their meal that Rosemary remembered the fish and chip shop in the village. Dogs would sometimes eat fish, and she persuaded Alec to fetch some cod for Spike. He made a terrific fuss about going, and did not relent until Rosemary said firmly that she would go herself.

By the time Alec returned, it was raining, and he was in a foul mood.

Determined not to be drawn into another quarrel, she whisked the fish into the kitchen, knowing the dog would follow. She left him thoroughly enjoying the pieces of fish, from which she had carefully removed all the batter. The poor creature looked as if he'd been kept short of food all his life, and she wished she could get her hands on the cruel man who had tied Spike up and left him to a lingering death.

'Satisfied, is he?' Alec's voice broke into her sombre thoughts, and she nodded absently.

'This idyllic rural backwater is clearly a bad influence on you,' he said firmly, taking her in his arms.

Just for a moment Rosemary was glad to rest her weary head on his broad shoulder, then reluctantly she eased herself out of his embrace. She had had a long, weary day, and needed all her strength for another long day tomorrow. She felt drained, unable even to respond to the man she had once loved, still loved. 'Forgive me, Alec,' she mur-

mured. 'I'm so tired I can't think straight, and——'
she began, but Alec kissed away the rest of the
words.

'I know just the cure for tiredness, my darling,'
he whispered in her ear. He swept her up in his
arms and carried her towards the stairs before she
was aware of what was happening.

'No! Alec, please!' Angrily she began to fight
him as he mounted the first stair.

Help came from an unexpected source. Seeing
his new friend apparently fighting for her life, Spike
gave an enormous leap, his great jaws catching
Alec's trouser leg.

Alec let out a bellow and nearly dropped Rosemary, who shrieked at Spike to let go. Man, woman
and dog collapsed on the stairs, and Rosemary tried
to calm the dog. It wasn't easy, because her sense of
humour came to the fore, and she could see the
funny side of the situation. Naturally Alec could
not, and he swore at Spike, as the dog hung on
grimly. Fortunately, it was only the material of the
trousers Spike was holding, not Alec's leg.

Alec began to tell Rosemary exactly what he
thought of her *and* her watchdog, but ignoring his
tirade she finally managed to get Spike's jaws open.

'Tomorrow, Rosemary,' Alec said tightly, 'you
will get rid of that Hound of the Baskervilles!
Either he goes—or I do,' he finished grimly.

'But Alec——' she began.

'I was hoping to spend the night here, but that's
obviously out of the question,' he went on, and
Rosemary's eyes sparked dangerously.

Ignoring the warning signs, if indeed he actually
saw them, Alec continued: 'I'm staying with your

aunt, and I'll be back tomorrow. Get rid of that dog before I return!' he ordered.

Rosemary opened her mouth to give him a long-overdue piece of her mind, but the doorbell rang peremptorily, and Spike howled.

'I'll go,' said Alec grimly. 'Don't these people know you're off duty?' He strode to the door, while Spike continued his baying, and Rosemary collapsed weakly into a chair. It had been one of those days and no mistake!

When she glanced up, her astonished gaze met that of Dr Craig Dean.

He stood beside Alec, and Rosemary's eyes went from one to the other. She was literally speechless. So, fortunately, was the dog. He stood protectively in front of her, as yet unsure of Craig's intentions.

'I didn't know you had company, Sister,' Craig said mildly. He held out the small cardboard box he was carrying. 'Steve told me he'd lumbered you with a stray dog, so . . . Six cans of dog food.'

Delighted, Rosemary took one of the cans. 'Here, boy—supper!' She held out the can to Spike, who wagged his tail.

Belatedly remembering her manners, she introduced the two men, then took the food through to the kitchen, an eager Spike bounding after her. He was happily working his way through half a can when she left him. She didn't want the men to be together for long. With two such uncompromising characters, sparks would fly before long!

There were no sparks, only a frigid silence. The iciness emanated from Alec, for Craig seemed quite at home, warming his hands before the fire.

He turned at Rosemary's entrance, and she

thanked him politely for the dog food. 'He's happy now. He wasn't as hungry as you might have expected,' she added. 'Alex bought him some fish at the fish shop.' She gave Alec a sweet smile, hoping to chase away the fit of the sullens which Craig's arrival had caused, but was only partially successful.

Alec smiled tightly. 'Rosemary is adept at getting her own way. You'll have to watch out, Doctor —she'll be taking over your practice in no time!'

That crooked, winsome smile crossed Craig's face, and Rosemary thought again how attractive it was. If only the man's character matched up to the pleasantness of his smile!

'Women are always adept at manipulation,' he said mildly. 'I intend to keep Sister Miller firmly in her place,' he added, and Rosemary's smile faded. Politeness held her silent, but her eyes spoke volumes.

Ignoring the explosive silence, Craig explained that he was on his way home. He was late home, even for a GP, and her rancour evaporated. The poor man must be tired out.

'Would you like some coffee, Doctor? I was just about to make some when you rang,' she lied, flushing a little as she remembered exactly what they *were* doing!

He accepted with an alacrity that surprised her. She saw Alec's mouth tighten, but surely he realised it was the least she could do? Dr Dean *was* her boss, in a way. GPs worked long hours, were just as subject to pressure as hospital doctors. More so, in a way, because they were on their own. Life-and-death decisions had to be made on the

spur of the moment, without the hospital back-up.
The man was desperately tired, even she could see
that. The fact that she didn't really like him had
nothing to do with it. Doctors must be cossetted,
her years in hospital nursing had taught her that.
When it came to it, theirs was the final decision,
they carried the burden.

She saw him glance at Alec's torn trouser leg, but
fortunately he did not comment. She wasn't sure
what she could have said to him!

Spike was searching hopefully for more food, so
Rosemary scooped out the rest of the can, while
Craig Dean watched, a faint smile on his face.

'Steve has taken advantage of your good nature,
Sister,' he said softly, and Rosemary shrugged.

'There was nothing else I could do—Mrs Abbott
wouldn't have the dog at home. Do you suppose
you could persuade her?' She turned to him, surprising a look of tenderness on his face.

There was a moment of silence, and Rosemary's
heart started beating erratically. Alec lounged in
the doorway, supposedly watching Spike, but
Rosemary wasn't deceived. He didn't trust Craig,
which was ridiculous. It wasn't as if she fancied the
man!

'I'll see if Lyn will reconsider,' the doctor agreed,
a gleam of amusement in his eyes. 'Are you a
dog-lover, Mr Scott?'

Alec was caught off guard. 'I—well, no, I'm not.
That creature bit me. Look!'

To Rosemary's consternation, Alec held up his
leg for Craig's inspection. 'He didn't actually catch
the flesh,' he admitted after a moment, 'but his
saliva must be full of bacteria!'

Alec sat down while Craig gravely inspected the trouser leg. Rosemary, hardly knowing whether to laugh or cry, busied herself with the coffee.

Still licking his lips, Spike went over to inspect Alec's leg for himself, but the doctor waved him away.

'You've done enough damage for one day, old fellow,' he said affably. To Rosemary's surprise, the dog lay down obediently, with one wary eye on Alec.

'You've escaped injury,' Craig announced. 'And unless the dog has rabies, you're safe from any bacteria. He didn't actually bite you.'

There was a trace of grim humour in his voice, and Rosemary kept her face averted, afraid lest she should burst out laughing.

'Is he a vicious dog?' Craig asked.

'Oh, no! He's very friendly,' she insisted.

He frowned, glancing from her to Alec and back again. 'Odd he should attack your friend,' he remarked, bending down to ruffle the dog's fur.

He didn't stay long, but Rosemary felt he would have if she'd been alone. Once or twice his eyes half closed, as if he was too weary to stay awake, and Rosemary felt a stab of sympathy for him.

'Is the whooping cough worse?' she ventured, as he rose to go.

He shook his head, then ran his fingers through his untidy fair hair. It was so long, particularly at the back, that once or twice Rosemary's fingers had itched to cut it for him. If they were alone now, she might well have offered; she had her scissors handy.

'No, there isn't much as yet. Don't worry, Sister,'

he smiled, 'we'll find plenty of cases for you before the year is out!'

'Sister might not be staying that long,' Alec said smoothly, and Rosemary nearly choked.

Craig eyed him thoughtfully. 'I hope you aren't trying to prise her away from us.' His voice was calm, but there was an edge to it that Rosemary didn't miss. 'I value her services greatly, Mr Scott. My need is greater than yours, I think.'

With that, he let himself out, leaving an uncomfortable silence behind.

Alec left soon after, but not before he had given Rosemary back her engagement ring.

He pressed the ring into her unwilling hand, and she stared down at its myriad sparkling stones—a sapphire surrounded by diamonds, a smaller version of the Princess of Wales's engagement ring. Once she had worn it so proudly. Yet that was before Alec's increasing infidelity had torn her apart.

'Allow me.' Deftly he turned her hand over, and slid the beautiful ring into place. 'That's where it belongs,' he said firmly.

Rosemary gazed up at him, her grey eyes full of sadness. 'Alec . . . I don't know what to say,' she murmured.

'Don't say anything, my love. Wear the ring, for my sake. I'll buy a gold chain and you can thread it through it for when you're on duty,' he offered, as he prepared to leave.

Rosemary, still wearing the ring, saw him out. He bent to give her a good night kiss, but Spike gave a warning growl, and, with a heartfelt sigh, Alec hurried out.

She wagged an admonishing finger at Spike. Clearly, *one* of the men in her life would have to go! Finding a home for Alec might be easier than finding one for Spike, but she would try.

The remainder of the week varied from busy to frantic. The problem of Spike still remained, and it crossed Rosemary's mind that Dr Dean might give the dog a home. Presumably he lived alone, and a watchdog would be useful. When she tentatively broached the subject, he chuckled.

'Me? I thought Spike was happy with you. Why on earth should he want to live with me?'

'He doesn't. *I* want him to live with you,' Rosemary said flatly.

'Nonsense, Rosemary. A watchdog is just what you need—it can be lonely here in the winter.' He raised a brow. 'Or will you be back in the Midlands before winter comes?'

'Of course I won't!' she said decisively. 'I've only just arrived. I haven't met all your patients yet, or even explored the countryside,' she went on, avoiding his gaze.

Alec's ring, suspended from a slender gold chain, hung about her neck under her uniform. For a small piece of jewellery it seemed to weigh a lot, and its presence was beginning to irk her. She could, of course, always take it off, but that would be treachery.

'We must do something about that.' Craig's voice broke into her sombre thoughts and she glanced up, startled.

'Yes, I was just thinking the same thing,' she

murmured, her mind still on the heavyweight engagement ring.

'I doubt if our thoughts were on the same problem, but never mind.' There was a note of sarcasm in his voice, and Rosemary tensed, hoping they weren't about to argue. So far this week they had been on remarkably good terms. Craig wasn't exactly friendly, but he hadn't snapped at her once.

'Shall we take Spike for a run through the Forest tomorrow afternoon? It's my half-day, and you can be spared for an hour, surely?' he suggested.

Rosemary's heart leapt. A brisk walk was exactly what she needed. It would blow the cobwebs away, help her come to a decision about Alec.

Thursday was clear and warm. They couldn't expect the heat of summer for their walk, but it certainly was an Indian summer, and Rosemary basked in the sunshine as she went briskly about her duties in the morning. As usual she arrived home just after one, to be greeted enthusiastically by Spike, who seemed to know a long walk was in the offing.

Craig called for her directly after lunch, and all three set out, Rosemary with a certain amount of diffidence. She was aware that he ought to be spending his half-day with Lyn Abbott.

At Craig's suggestion they set off in his car, Spike being firmly lodged on the back seat. Being a big dog, he could sit comfortably on the seat and still lean forward to join in the conversation, or to lick the back of Rosemary's neck.

Fortunately, the doctor made no more than a few general remarks, leaving Rosemary to her own thoughts. Absently she turned and stroked the dog, wishing she could get as close emotionally to Alec. For now there was a barrier between them, and that had helped her to come to a decision. She must return Alec's ring, explain to him that she needed time to sort herself out.

Craig's calm voice broke in her troubled thoughts. 'We get out here and walk. Come on, old fellow.'

Spike needed no second telling. He badly needed a really long walk, and Rosemary was glad to relinquish him into Craig's care. She had bought a collar and an extending lead so that he could gallop away to the extent of several feet, but she wouldn't risk letting him off the lead.

She gazed about her with interest. As yet she had had no time to explore, and she was glad to have a guide for her first foray.

'We're at the northern fringes of the Forest.' Craig answered her unspoken question, blue eyes thoughtful as they rested on her.

She pretended to look around for the dog. There was too much meaning in the doctor's gaze, and it was as if he knew she had been thinking about Alec. Perhaps he had X-ray eyes, like some Ward Sisters, and could see the ring suspended between her breasts!

A small sigh escaped her, and he took her hand, squeezing it gently.

'Come on, we've a long way to go.' His voice was tender, and she felt horribly guilty. He was being so kind, so understanding. Was it, though, a ploy? Would he trap her into thinking what a kind man he was, how considerate of her feelings, then, when she'd made up her mind to stay, would he change back into the arrogant, forceful doctor she'd met at first?

She pulled her hand free and walked slightly ahead of him. Spike's lead could be seen descending into some shrubbery, but his body was completely hidden.

'That road you can see over there is the main Eastbourne to Purley Road—the London road, I suppose you'd call it.' Craig's manner was brisk and matter-of-fact again, and Rosemary didn't know whether to be pleased or sorry.

'Where?' She craned her neck.

'You're looking in the wrong direction, Rosemary,' he said softly.

'But I'm not! That's where you——' She wasn't allowed to finish the sentence. As she glanced at him, his strong arms cradled her to his chest. Then, as he bent his head to kiss her, she raised her mouth to his. It was a purely involuntary gesture. Right then it seemed the most natural thing in the world for Craig to kiss her.

After what seemed an eternity, they broke apart. Rosemary was shaken, and that was putting it mildly!

If she expected him to apologise, she was disappointed. Indeed, the doctor seemed totally unmoved by what Rosemary had found an earth-shattering experience. 'Where's that dog got to?' he muttered. 'Spike! Here, boy!'

She closed her eyes in momentary disbelief, as Craig whistled to the dog, then she heard Spike's enthusiastic bark as Craig reeled in the lead. He was completely unaffected by the kiss, unaware and uncaring that he had turned Rosemary's life upside down.

Pulling herself together with an effort, she bent down to pat the dog. She was hurt and angry. How dared he throw a casual kiss her way! It meant no more to him than throwing a stick for the dog to retrieve. He was heartless!

'Rosemary?'

Startled, she glanced up. She hadn't heard him move. Blue eyes searched hers as if seeking confirmation that she'd received the kiss as lightly as he'd given it.

She forced a bright smile to her lips. It wasn't easy, for she felt as if she never wanted to smile again. 'Spike's certainly enjoying himself, Doctor,' she said briskly. 'Thank you for bringing us.' She made an elaborate show of glancing at her watch, afraid lest he see the misery that she could not completely hide. Then the hurt, the heartache, overwhelmed her, and she could keep up the pretence no longer. 'Isn't one woman enough for you?' she burst out, startling herself as well as him. '*Must* you sample every reasonably young woman who comes your way?'

He stared at her, while she sought for control. Of course, she wasn't berating him at all; it was Alec's sins she was visiting on the doctor. Yet he had no right to kiss her, not with Lyn Abbott's little boy calling him 'Daddy'! She'd thought him a better man than Alec, and it was bitter medicine to have to admit her mistake.

She bit back the tears, feeling foolish. 'I . . . I'm sorry, Doctor. It's just that—' She broke off, and bent to fondle Spike, who was staring at her, as much surprised as Craig, probably.

'It's just that your ex-lover spreads his favours around and now you think *I'm* going to,' Craig finished the sentence for her.

'No, he doesn't!' she protested, then stopped when she saw the sceptical expression on his face. 'He *does* fool around,' she admitted. 'That's why I broke off our engagement. I couldn't take any more. I kept turning a blind eye when friends told me about . . . about his affairs, but there comes a time when you *have* to face reality,' she whispered, not expecting him to understand.

But he did understand. Gently he stroked her cheek. She tensed, half wanting, half not wanting, him to touch her.

'I know what it's like, Rosemary,' he said tenderly. 'Love never quite dies, no matter how illogical that love. One part of your heart always belongs to that special person.'

Eagerly she clutched his arm. 'That's it! I *do* love Alec, yet . . . I just don't know how much more heartache I can take.'

'Send him away, Rosemary. Time will take care of the heartache,' he advised.

Their eyes met, and what she saw in his caused her heart to flutter. Perhaps he *did* care for her a little. That kiss hadn't been as light and idle as she'd believed.

Of course, she could never love Craig Dean. Her heart belonged to Alec, perhaps for ever. She was comforted, though, by the knowledge that Craig understood her problem, and that the kiss had meant something to them both.

CHAPTER FIVE

ON THE drive back, Craig offered to take Rosemary one day to the Poohsticks Bridge, so beloved of A. A. Milne and his characters.

'Pooh and Christopher Robin used to play there, though it isn't actually within the Forest. Lyn might come, too,' he added casually, and she agreed that Lyn might indeed come.

Whatever attraction Rosemary might have for the doctor, his heart belonged to Lyn. Perhaps she had let him down in the past. That must have been what he meant when he said that love never quite died.

They were almost back in Hurstfield when they were flagged down. A man was running along the road towards them, waving as he came. It was a little-used road, and Rosemary had seen no other cars for miles.

The man came panting up. 'There's been an accident! Can you—Oh, thank God it's you, Doctor!' He mopped his perspiring brow, and continued his story inside the car. A girl motor-cyclist had crashed into a tree outside his isolated house. There was no other traffic about and no telephone nearby.

'I did what I could. She was conscious, Doctor,' he panted, as Craig drove along, seeking the turn-off towards the man's house.

They found the young motor-cyclist sitting up,

glancing around in a dazed fashion, and Rosemary went forward to help her.

Her helmet was lying on the ground beside her, and as Rosemary came up to her, the casualty lay down again as if too weary to care.

Craig performed a quick examination, then sent Rosemary off in his car to seek a telephone. 'The village will be the best place, Rosemary,' he ordered. 'Don't stop at any houses, that'll only waste valuable time. The nearest phonebox is in the opposite direction to Hurstfield.'

Fortunately, it wasn't a matter of life and death, yet the girl worried Rosemary. She had bruising to the face and must have hit her face and perhaps her head when she fell. The helmet might not have deflected all the blow. At the very least, her brain would have received a good shaking.

Rosemary arrived back at the scene of the accident just before the ambulance. Craig had made the girl as comfortable as possible but hadn't moved her. The helpful owner of the house had placed the warning triangles from Craig's car on the road, and stood ready to head off any vehicle that might approach. Rosemary had seen the speed at which motorists drove through the main roads that bisected the Forest, and thought the girl was lucky to be lying in the middle of a country lane, well off the tourist track.

Their casualty was fully conscious now, but possible head injury could not be ruled out. In addition, she had fractured her left arm, and Craig had splinted it roughly. Her eyes were full of pain, though, and Rosemary offered what comfort she could.

They followed the ambulance to the General, an abnormally subdued Spike lying on the back seat, perhaps feeling left out of all the excitement.

The girl was local, and while Craig was at the hospital, Rosemary volunteered to seek out the parents and put them in the picture. After her errand of mercy was accomplished, she walked back towards the village, but must have taken a wrong turning.

Wishing she had taken up Craig's offer of his car, she retraced her steps. Yet to a stranger, one winding country lane looked much the same as all the rest, and she ended up going round in a circle. She had taken the precaution of tying her distinctive scarf to a tree before she tried the second lane, and could have wept when she came back to the same tree.

Her red and white scarf fluttered bravely in the strengthening breeze, and she was glad of its warmth. Pulling her anorak hood over her head and silently cursing her stupidity, she set out once more. She had given up hope of finding a way out of the Forest, but she knew she was bound to find an occupied cottage sooner or later.

Quite *why* she didn't see the ditch, she wasn't sure. Perhaps fatigue could be blamed. She chose to blame Craig Dean for the fact that she fell into the ditch. She also blamed him, out loud, for all the other misfortunes she'd suffered since coming to Ashdown Forest.

It was then that she remembered Lyn Abbott. Remembered, too, Granny Cole's words about not taking anything Lyn wanted for herself.

Rosemary went cold. Although dusk was

drawing in, her coldness was due to more than the chill of the day. It was incredibly stupid of her to think, even for a moment, that Lyn was responsible for her troubles, and she pushed the thought away. Yet it made her uneasy, and she could have cried with relief when she at last found the road into Hurstfield.

The mud on her shoes from the ditch caused her to slip, and her relief turned to horror as she measured her length on the road.

The lights from an approaching vehicle was the last thing she saw before she momentarily lost consciousness . . .

She could hear Craig's voice calling her from afar. It was a few moments before she realised that he wasn't far away at all, he was bending over her, eyes full of concern.

She strenuously resisted when he suggested she go to hospital for a check-up. 'Definitely not, Doctor. I'm fine. It was weariness more than anything. I didn't hit my head, I'm just shaken – and bruised in places I'd rather not mention!' she added, with a touch of wry humour, and he grinned.

'Right, we'll all go home now. I could do with a cup of coffee, and I expect Spike will want another bite to eat!'

Despite Rosemary's protests, he scooped her up in his arms and carried her to his car. If her head hadn't been aching so much, she would have enjoyed the contact. His tweed jacket smelt faintly of after-shave.

She closed her eyes again, then opened them a fraction, hardly able to believe that she was in Craig Dean's arms. *Was* it Dr Dean? She noted the firm, rather square jaw and wide mouth. Yes, it was him. Comforted, she closed her eyes again, and did not wake until the car stopped.

Craig helped her out of the roomy car, supporting her as she walked up the three steep steps to the front door. Her brain barely registered the fact that there was only one step to her front door, then they were inside. Warmth enveloped her, then she realised: it was the doctor's house. Central heating was a luxury her cottage lacked.

Spike, however, seemed at home. He immediately jumped on to the long, low leather settee in front of a log fire. Dr Dean shooed him off, as he laid Rosemary down on to the settee.

'I'll get a rug. Make yourself at home,' he called over his shoulder, and she adjusted her position a little so that she could watch him stride from the room. She found two big cushions and made herself as comfortable as she could, then he was back with a couple of blankets and a quilt.

He paused in the doorway for a moment, and Rosemary, eyes half closed, was able to survey him from under her long golden-brown lashes. He *still* needed a haircut. Still needed someone to press his shirt as well, and his jeans had seen better days. He needed taking in hand, she decided. It was time Lyn put her own problems to one side and concentrated on the man she supposedly loved. If anyone needed tender loving care, it was Dr Dean!

She ought not to be here. She felt she was usurping Lyn's place, and a shadow crossed her face.

Craig misinterpreted her expression. 'I don't

suppose he'll worry too much, Rosemary. He probably thinks there's an epidemic of bubonic plague in the village.' His tone was curt, dismissive, and she flushed angrily.

She made no comment, however. No good would come from arguing with the man. He must always be right.

Because Spike wouldn't leave her, she had to leave the comfort of the settee and accompany him to the kitchen, where a plate of food was placed before him. She sat in an ancient rocking chair, and Craig tucked the quilt around her. While he put the coffee on to percolate, Rosemary was free to glance about her.

The kitchen was much bigger than hers. A long room, it had a breakfast bar at the other end, next to what she assumed was a larder. Labour-saving gadgets took up the rest of the space, and her eyes gleamed at the sight of the modern automatic washing machine. Why, he even had a dishwasher!

She eyed him in mock reproach as he set out a plate of petits fours. 'You've got all these lovely washing aids! I could cry,' she added candidly. 'I have to make do with a small spin-drier. There isn't room for anything else, not even a washing machine.'

'The gadgets came with the house, actually,' Craig admitted a little later, as they sipped their coffee. 'I rent this place furnished—complete with all mod cons, as the estate agents say! I don't know how I would manage otherwise—there's no local laundry.'

It crossed her mind that Lyn ought to do his

washing, but she bit back the words. No doubt Lyn had enough to do.

Before they left, Craig took her on a guided tour of the house, with Spike padding along at their heels.

Although spacious and filled with good-quality furniture, the house lacked character, Rosemary felt. It wasn't a home, it did not appear lived in—but then it probably wasn't lived in much, she reflected sadly. Craig Dean was a busy man.

Yet it was more than just lack of time. She stood in the sun lounge, which ran the whole length of the rear elevation, and pondered the matter. The house, for all its tidiness, was neglected. It needed a family. It needed a woman's touch.

It had a woman's touch, to some extent, for he had mentioned his housekeeper. She was a retired nanny, who lived with her husband at the other end of the village. 'She comes in most days,' he commented.

'Does your housekeeper get meals for you?' Rosemary asked as she idly picked up a potted cyclamen. The sun lounge was full of them, and they probably belonged to the housekeeper.

'Sometimes. Or Lyn does,' he admitted. 'Either I eat there or she comes here, or the Tunstalls invite me for a meal.'

Rosemary nodded silently. She ought to be pleased that Lyn took *some* interest in his welfare. Funnily enough, she wasn't pleased, and the fact worried her. She didn't want the man to starve, and *she* could hardly be expected to feed him.

Thoughtfully, she replaced the plant and turned to follow him out of the sun lounge. 'How is Lyn's problem?' she asked. 'Her husband, I mean.'

He grimaced. 'Peter wouldn't thank you for calling him a problem! I think—given time—everything will come to a satisfactory conclusion. We're hoping so, anyway.'

'Yes, naturally,' Rosemary agreed. Once the divorce was through and the custody of the boy settled, Craig Dean would be able to marry Lyn. Steve would have a real father then, a man who would care for him, watch over him as he grew, set him a good example.

A wave of nostalgia overcame her, a kind of homesickness for her own father. Steve would be lucky to have such a father as Craig Dean.

'Why so sad?' he queried.

'What? Oh, I was just dwelling on the past,' she admitted. It was foolish and she knew it. A big, strapping woman like her didn't need a parent! 'I was thinking you would make a good father for Steve,' she added, since he seemed to be expecting her to say more.

'Oh? The way Scott is for you?' There was a trace of amusement in his voice, and she resented it.

'No! I don't think of him as a father.' He's just—well . . . He's mature, a sophisticated man of the world,' she said crossly. 'He's hardly a father figure.'

'He's too old for you, Rosemary,' he said decisively. 'Too old, too sophisticated, wrong in every way.'

Rosemary gasped. This was going too far! 'You're exceeding the bounds of good manners, Dr Dean,' she said tightly.

He raised one of those devilish brows, and his

very blue eyes caught and held her gaze. 'The truth always hurts, Rosemary. One day you'll see that I'm right.'

'I can't imagine why you should concern yourself, Doctor. My love life isn't your business.'

'Perhaps it isn't, but if your "mature man of the world" is going to drag you back to the bright lights, then it does become my business. We can't have staff leaving before they've even settled into the job.'

'No, of course not, Doctor,' she agreed. Put that way, his interest in Alec Scott's intentions was perfectly reasonable.

'Will you stop calling me Doctor! Doctor this and Doctor that! It irritates me,' he added unnecessarily.

'Everything I do irritates you!' she snapped back. 'Perhaps I'd be doing us both a good turn by marrying Alec and leaving you!'

'I don't intend that you should ever leave me, Rosemary.' His tone was soft, seductive almost, and she retreated a step. The change in his manner worried her, but then he often worried her! A chameleon would have fewer changes.

Hastily she got up, the rocking chair creaking as she did so. 'I expect I ought to make a move, doctor. There were one or two visits I didn't get around to.' Her tone was reproachful, but it wasn't really his fault. She had enjoyed most of the afternoon and could always catch up tomorrow. If necessary, she could work part of Saturday.

'Call me Craig,' he suggested, a smile hovering about his mouth. 'After all, we're off duty. I'll see you home.'

Craig. Silently she practised saying the name. Yes, it had a masculine ring to it, suggesting someone dependable, tough . . .

She eyed him thoughtfully when he returned after collecting his jacket. He *was* dependable, of course. Trustworthy, a man to turn to in a crisis . . . The strong jaw and firm mouth suggested a trace of ruthlessness in his make-up, as well. A man not to be trifled with.

He saw her safely inside the cottage, but was clearly anxious to get away.

Rosemary tried not to show her disappointment. After all, he was a busy man and she'd taken up enough of his time already.

He paused in the doorway, his gaze sad. 'Remember what I said, Rosemary, about Scott not being right for you. I don't want to see you hurt.'

Touched, she laid her hand on his arm. 'I've been hurt already, Craig. I don't intend to let him bruise my heart again.'

'Sensible girl,' he smiled, before bending his head to kiss her.

Startled, Rosemary held back for a moment, while the dog looked on with interest. Craig's grip tightened, and she relaxed against him, returning the kiss. Craig nuzzled her ear, and her arms crept about his neck, pulling his head down.

'Oh, Rosemary,' he murmured, sounding dazed. Then Spike gave a gigantic yawn, and it was that which brought them down to earth again.

'I'd better go. Good night,' he said abruptly, and Rosemary was alone.

She sat down on the settee and stared into the artificial flames of the fire. Conjuring up a picture of Craig Dean was deceptively easy, but trying to escape from the picture was almost impossible.

As she tidied the little cottage, scenes from their afternoon together came to haunt her: the calm yet decisive way Craig dealt with the emergency, his words 'I don't intend you should leave me', his winsome smile . . .

It came almost as a relief when Alec phoned. She had just bathed and was ready to climb the stairs to her chilly bedroom.

Alec was angry, unjustifiably so, she felt. 'I've phoned *three* times, Rosemary!' he bellowed the moment she picked up the telephone. 'I couldn't get down today, and——'

'I've been on duty, Alec.' She kept her voice calm.

'Are you *sure* you've been on duty?'

His words caught her off guard. 'Well—yes! Yes, of course I have. Oh, no . . . Spike and I went——'

'Spike or Dr Dean?'

'Both,' she said firmly. 'Dr Dean took us for a ride and——'

'I'll bet he did! You took the afternoon off to go joy-riding with that man leaving me to worry about you all afternoon and evening! You can't have been driving all evening, surely? I suppose you stopped for dinner in some cosy rural nook?' Alec's voice dripped sarcasm, but Rosemary ignored it.

They *didn't* stop for dinner in some rural nook, nor did Craig Dean invite her for a meal at his house. That must mean he was expected at Lyn Abbott's for his evening meal. He wouldn't want to refuse, let Lyn know he was dining out with his district nurse.

'No, we came straight back after the accident,' she said matter-of-factly. 'Who told you the doctor gave me a lift?'

'*What* accident?' Alec demanded, ignoring her question, and she gave him brief details, all the time wondering who *did* tell him that she'd spent the afternoon with Craig Dean.

He hurriedly asked her how she was, but she cut him short, replacing the receiver while he was in mid-sentence. She'd had enough.

On Friday she was kept busy every moment, and when she had no work, she made some. Just before lunch she paid a flying visit to the surgery. She had been there once already, for the regular Friday briefings. To her surprise, Lyn Abbott had not been present, but she couldn't tell from Craig Dean's manner whether the woman was ill, or simply busy elsewhere. No one mentioned her.

Gwen Sayers beamed at Rosemary on her second visit. 'Been keeping you busy, have they? Sister Pearson always used to say she never had a minute!'

'Sister Pearson was right. I may have to catch up with my visits tomorrow,' Rosemary said. 'Here's my list for this afternoon. Is there anyone on the list who mustn't be visited on a Saturday? I know it's market day in——'

'On a Saturday?' echoed Gwen. 'Leave them till Monday, I should. Oh, of course—you took yesterday afternoon off! Went joy-riding with the young doctor!' Gwen beamed even more, but Rosemary went cold.

'Did I go joy-riding, Gwen?'

Gwen leaned forward and lowered her voice. *'She* saw you,' she said in a hoarse whisper, and Rosemary knew at once who she meant. 'That's why she isn't in today. Can't bear to see him taking an interest in another woman,' she finished tartly.

Rosemary tried to keep her voice light. Helpful though she was, Gwen was an incorrigible gossip, and it wouldn't do to say anything which might get back to Lyn. 'I'm sure Lyn doesn't regard me as "another woman" in quite the way you mean.' Her tone brooked no argument, and Gwen looked disappointed. 'Dr Dean invited Spike and myself out for a walk, and that's what we had. Then we met up with an accident.' She sketched the details for the receptionist, hoping to divert her mind from the drive with Dr Dean.

She had found time to check up on the young motor-cyclist. Although neurological tests at the General Hospital had found no apparent brain damage, the girl was still far from right, and was to be transferred to the Regional Neurological Centre.

Rosemary wondered briefly if Gwen had been responsible for telling Alec where she was, but dismissed the thought. It wasn't important now, anyway.

Her next visit was to be to the Fairleys, who lived in a cottage on a small farm to the north of the village. They were a rather feckless, happy-go-lucky family, and Rosemary had taken to them immediately.

It was late afternoon by the time she got there, and she hoped there would be a cup of tea waiting. They were an hospitable family, as were most in the village. She no longer felt a stranger. She belonged to the village now—well, *almost* belonged. It would take months if not years before she was fully assimilated.

There was no one at home, but a passing farm-worker told her that Mrs Fairley had taken Mandy to the dentist. Presumably the pre-school children had gone, too.

Mention of Mandy Fairley made Rosemary determined to pop in to see the family over the weekend. Her visits were to dress the ulcer on Mrs Fairley's leg, but apart from the asthmatic boy, there was the fourteen-year-old girl, Mandy, with what Rosemary half suspected was anorexia nervosa. That was a disorder she did not expect to find in the heart of the country. It was sometimes brought on by stress, and she wondered what might have stressed the girl out here in the glorious countryside.

She had met many cases of anorexia nervosa during her inner-city work, and had always found its aetiology fascinating. There was so much that could be done to help the sufferers, if only they would co-operate.

She smiled sadly as she drove back to her cottage. She had a feeling the Fairleys were going to loom large in her life in the coming weeks, but that was what district nursing was all about.

It was strange, but she'd had such a full day that she hadn't thought about Alec, even once.

The doctors took turns to provide a Saturday morning surgery, and Rosemary knew it was Craig's turn this weekend. She intended asking his advice about the Fairleys. Alec was taking her out to lunch, but she would be back in good time.

She didn't expect to see Lyn at the surgery and had forgotten to check the rota to see which receptionist was on duty. She smiled warmly at the woman, wondering what sort of response she would get. She couldn't help remembering Gwen's words about Lyn seeing her out with Dr Dean.

Lyn greeted her with a faint smile. She was even paler than usual, and Rosemary longed to offer her comfort. What sort of comfort, she wasn't sure; it was presumptuous of her to believe she could cure everyone's ills, physical or emotional.

Craig came in before Rosemary had time to do more than comment on the weather. He surveyed her quizzically. 'Are you on call, Sister? I thought it was Sister Gasson from the other practice?'

'It is, but I wanted to see you about the Fairleys, Doctor.' No way would she call him Craig in front of his girl-friend! 'I'm going to pop in to see them this morning, then I've one or two calls left over from Thursday,' she admitted.

She saw the look Lyn gave Craig, and could have bitten out her tongue. Why on earth did she have to mention the calls left over? It would remind Lyn that she'd spent part of Thursday gadding about the countryside with the doctor, when she ought to have been working.

Mentally shrugging, she followed him into his consulting room, being careful to leave the door open so that the receptionist would not feel excluded.

After she had given him details of several other

patients, she mentioned the Fairley daughter with possible anorexia nervosa.

'Oh, that one! Yes, that's Mandy, I think.' He smiled. 'I forget which is which. I know three of them are girls. Mrs Fairley aborted just before you came—that would have made seven altogether.'

'This girl is taller than the rest, and she's got strong, stringy blonde hair,' Rosemary put in. 'She's rather a pretty girl otherwise. I was surprised to find anorexia nervosa out here and——'

'We do have a *few* city diseases,' Craig pointed out with a faint smile, and Rosemary coloured. 'It isn't all A. A. Milne and Christopher Robin,' he added dryly.

Rosemary chuckled. 'No, Doctor,' she said demurely.

That little smile she found so attractive was hovering about his mouth, but this morning it annoyed her for some reason. She left as soon as she could, being careful to say a few words to Lyn on the way out. No way must she add jealousy to the woman's problems.

She called at the hospital to see another patient, then drove up to the farm. After seeing the Fairleys, she fitted in the two postponed visits, then stopped for a late coffee in Hurstfield.

The village was just big enough to contain two supermarkets yet small enough to be friendly. It seemed to her that everyone knew everyone else, and she sat idly watching the passersby. The sun came streaming in through the window of the café, and Rosemary felt at peace with the world.

Then she remembered: Alec would be waiting. A cloud crossed the sun, but it might have only been her imagination. Alec, the man she loved, the man she was going the marry.

With a sigh, she rose. It wouldn't do to idle here; they were to spend the afternoon together and probably the evening as well.

Deep in thought, she passed the ancient market cross, recalling Gwen's remark about it being a favourite trysting place for young lovers. It sounded so romantic, and she paused, wondering how many youngsters were waiting there for their partners.

Lyn Abott did not qualify as a youngster, but she was waiting under the granite cross. There was an archway underneath, and Lyn and her son were standing there, clearly waiting for someone.

Rosemary's heart began to ache, and she turned and walked briskly back the way she had come. It was time to meet Alec.

She didn't know why she told Alec later that she couldn't marry him. Seeing Lyn Abbott waiting patiently for Craig Dean could have had no bearing on her decision. It was just that she suddenly knew she could not go through with the renewed engagement, let alone a wedding.

After Alec had slammed out of the cottage, Rosemary sank down on to the settee and sobbed her heart out. As though he understood her distress, Spike leapt on to the settee and began to nuzzle her.

Smiling through the tears, Rosemary hugged him. Spike was better company than any number of men. She was finished with men for ever!

CHAPTER SIX

FOR the next few days, Rosemary was subdued and unhappy and she saw Craig glance quizzically at her once or twice. She wasn't actually depressed, but sending away the man you had once loved was nothing to be cheerful about.

Of course, the patients noticed nothing. They had worries enough of their own without trying to ease the burdens of the district nurse. Most patients, she felt, did not realise that doctors and nurses had problems of their own.

Mr Krender died at last, and Rosemary attended his funeral, her own troubles seeming slight now. Later, she went to visit Granny Cole, as much out of a desire to be cheered up as anything. She could understand why her predecessor had liked visiting the old lady.

Although as cheerful as ever, Mrs Cole had a cold. 'Can't seem to shake it off, Sister,' she sniffed. 'Still, at my age you have to expect ailments most of the year.'

She sounded chesty, and Rosemary offered to call in Dr Dean, but the old lady waved away the suggestion. 'The chemist in the village will make me up a bottle of summat good!' she chuckled. 'I gets this every winter.'

'Lyn doesn't seem well, either.' Rosemary wasn't sure why she mentioned Lyn; perhaps there was the faint hope at the back of her mind that she might reconcile the grandmother and grand-daughter.

The old woman shrugged. 'She's an odd girl, always has been. That husband of hers didn't help matters, but she could have got worse.'

'Do you think they'll get back together?' Rosemary was unaware of the eagerness in her voice until the patient commented on it.

'Wanting them to kiss and make up, are you?' Mrs Cole went on shrewdly, and Rosemary didn't know where to put her face.

'It would be better for Steve's sake,' she muttered. 'He needs a father. Every boy does.'

'I expect he'll find one eventually. Lyn's a good-looking woman, if I says so as shouldn't!'

'Yes, there's that,' Rosemary agreed. 'Of course he calls Dr Dean "Daddy", so I suppose he's hoping Dr Dean will be his new father.'

Granny Cole looked astonished. '*Does* he? That's a shrewd move on Lyn's part!' she cackled, then was overcome by a fit of coughing.

Rosemary frowned, determined to get the old lady to the surgery if Craig hadn't time to visit. Granny was all alone and it worried her, even if it didn't worry the patient.

Craig agreed to visit Mrs Cole before the end of the week, and Rosemary intended looking in on her again before then. Craig would probably go when he was officially off duty, since he too enjoyed her company. The village people tended to stick together and help one another, at least those who had lived there all their lives, and Mrs Cole wasn't without friends. Someone popped in every day, she assured Rosemary.

Yet Rosemary was still troubled. The house was so far out of the village and would be difficult to reach if the snows came. Hypothermia would be as much a problem here as in more urban areas. Could she, *dared* she mention the problem to Lyn? Surely it would be a good way of getting the two of them together? In any case, Steve ought not to be deprived of his great-grandmother. Never having known a grandmother, let alone a great-grandmother, Rosemary had felt the loss keenly.

For that reason, she was determined that Steve should have the granny she could not have herself. Rosemary had emerged from a very lonely childhood as a surprisingly popular woman. She had plenty of friends, loved and was loved by her Aunt Lizzie, but nothing could make up for the loss of proper family life, she felt.

She and Lyn were in Craig Dean's consulting room when she tentatively mentioned Granny Cole.

'She's a bit wheezy,' Rosemary went on, fair head bent over some notes. Craig was on his rounds, and it was pleasantly cosy sitting in his chair. She yawned and stretched, eyeing Lyn speculatively.

Lyn's expression was as difficult to read as ever, and Rosemary ploughed on: 'I've asked Dr Dean to look in on her, but she really needs company, I think. Someone living in there,' she added.

There was a flicker of what might have been amusement in Lyn's gaze. Greenish eyes watched Rosemary carefully, as if waiting to pounce.

'What I'm trying to say is that your gran would

appreciate a visit from you.' There, it was out. No more cat-and-mouse games.

She met Lyn's cool gaze, wondering what response she would get. 'Do you think you might visit her, Lyn? Just for ten minutes, you and Steve?'

'I shouldn't think so.' Lyn turned away coldly, and Rosemary lost her temper.

They were arguing when Gwen Sayers arrived. On hearing Gwen, Rosemary bit back what she had been about to say. She had already said more than enough, and none of it had apparently penetrated the invisible armour that Lyn Abbott wore permanently.

Although she must have seen Gwen arrive, Lyn wasn't prepared to temporarily bury the hatchet, except perhaps in Rosemary's head. 'I think you're the most obnoxious, interfering district nurse Craig has had!' she said clearly and loudly. 'That Pearson woman was bad enough, but you think you can come here with your big city ways, telling us how to manage our affairs! What business is it of yours? You can't even manage your own love life, so why don't you leave *me* alone? And Craig too,' she rushed on, before Rosemary could comment.

She swept out, past Gwen, and out through the main door, leaving Rosemary feeling worse than she would have believed possible.

Lyn was right: she had no business instructing people. They had managed perfectly well before she came and would manage once she left. At that moment she felt that leaving was all she wanted to do.

Rosemary had just returned to her cottage the following lunchtime when she saw Craig's car draw up. Spike barked encouragingly, but Rosemary didn't feel like company. She'd had a bad morning. Mrs Tuppin, the leukaemia sufferer, was worse, frailer and more tired. She laughed off Rosemary's concern and assured her it was just 'a touch of the blood pressure', but the patient was clearly weaker, and she was such a sweet soul. It would be awful if she didn't live to see another Christmas, as she and her husband were such a devoted couple. Her husband did what he could, but he lacked finesse and imagination, Rosemary felt, but acknowledged that she might have been unfair to the man. She couldn't expect *every* man to have the understanding and compassion of Craig Dean. Or of Dr Tunstall, come to that. Although a trifle austere on the surface, the older doctor was well liked by his patients. She had one of his to visit directly after lunch, and she hoped the old doctor's nephew wasn't about to detain her.

No, the old doctor's nephew wasn't going to detain her, he was going to wipe the floor with her instead!

He started on her the moment she opened the door. Her welcoming smile faded, and she backed away from his anger.

'I've had Lyn weeping on my shoulder this morning!' he snarled. 'You know she's having a bad time! What on earth possessed you to mention Granny Cole?'

Rosemary's anger grew to match his. 'Mrs Cole happens to be Lyn's grandmother, and I thought it would do the old lady good to have a visit from——'

'Who are you to tell people what's good for

them? Who gave you the authority to interfere in Lyn's private life?'

He no longer appeared angry, but it was there, just below the surface. He had himself well under control now, and only the flinty expression in his eyes warned her that there was more to come.

Rosemary had no excuse to offer, except that she had been thinking only of what was best for Mrs Cole. Tilting her determined jaw a bit higher, she told him firmly that Lyn was making a fuss over nothing. 'If I upset her, than I'm genuinely sorry,' she went on in a softer tone. 'But people with ultra-sensitive feelings are a pain sometimes. Whatever other people say or do, it's always wrong!'

Hands on hips, she glared at him. 'I'm fed up with Lyn doesn't like this, Lyn has had a tough time, Lyn's problems are too much for her, etc, etc! She certainly knows how to bring *you* to heel!' she added rashly, then stepped back a pace at the anger in his eyes.

'No one, but *no one*, brings me to heel, Sister Miller!' he snapped.

'No, Doctor,' she said penitently.

'In the short while you've been with us, you've achieved a great deal, Sister Miller,' he went on grimly.

'Yes, Doctor.' Rosemary hung her head and put her hands behind her back, linking her fingers together in the approved manner. 'I'm very sorry, Doctor,' she added for good measure.

When he didn't reply, she risked a glance at him. Their eyes met and she was relieved to see a glint of amusement there.

'You forgot to add "three bags full, Doctor". Your display of penitence should win you an Oscar,' he added.

'Yes, Doctor.' Her tone might not have been sufficiently humble, for he came nearer, reaching out a finger which he trailed gently down her cheek.

Mock penitence forgotten, she tensed, wondering why on earth his touch should affect her so much. Compared with Alec, he was very ordinary, a mere beginner in the seduction stakes. He might be good enough for the Lyn Abbotts of this world, but Rosemary Miller deserved a more sophisticated——

His mouth came down harshly on hers, and she forgot what sort of man she deserved. All she knew was that she wanted this one. She moaned in protest when his mouth left hers temporarily, then the moan became a sigh as his lips gently nuzzled her ear.

'I could get to enjoy this.' Craig spoke with his lips pressed against her throat. She silently endorsed his words when his teeth nibbled away at her earlobe.

'This is most unprofessional, Dr Dean,' she murmured, after another kiss. 'I shall report you to the union!'

'Spoilsport!' he chuckled. Then, with what might have been relief, he let her go, leaving her to find her own way to the armchair. She had enough of her senses unaddled to know that she mustn't stake herself out on the settee. That *would* be an invitation to more serious lovemaking!

Her body felt chilled after the heat they had generated between them, but they were both on duty, and she was conscious of the time passing. Duty called and must continue to call. Their work was all they could ever share. For Craig had Lyn Abbott, a millstone perhaps, but she was presumably the woman he loved. The dalliance with Sister Miller was just an episode to relieve the monotony. He must sometimes get tired of that weeping willow of a woman.

She watched him from under her lashes, as he rearranged his necktie. He looked even more of a mess. Although clean, his shirt and cords were old and creased.

'You still need a haircut,' she told him, rousing herself. 'I've got my duty scissors here. Shall I snip a few pieces off for you?' she asked, with a smile.

He chuckled. 'You're very obliging, but I think I ought to visit a barber. It's hardly a nursing duty.'

His expression was wary, his eyes hooded, and Rosemary died a little. Of course she had no right to cut his hair, choose his clothes, prepare his food . . . They were wifely duties, and Sister Miller was presumptuous in thinking she could take on any of those duties.

If she thought she'd been forgiven for upsetting Lyn, she was mistaken. Once on the doorstep, Craig delivered his final salvo. 'Remember, Rosemary, that nurses are supposed to provide tender loving care. Keep your interest strictly professional, and leave other people to get on with their own lives.'

Resentment burned in her breast, but she was honest enough to admit the truth of his remark. From now on, Sister Miller would confine herself strictly to ulcers, wounds, and injections! Trying to be helpful was clearly not appreciated.

Mandy Fairley was her last call that afternoon. Rosemary wanted to give her time to get home from school, but one of the younger boys told her that Mandy hadn't gone to school.

Wondering why, Rosemary walked into the house. Perhaps the girl's urine infection was worse. That was the official reason for the visit, to tell her the result of the tests on her urine specimen. The question of the possible anorexia nervosa was far more important, although the two could be connected. Anorexia nervosa sufferers developed physical complications after a time—various infections, anaemia, and so on. Eventually, of course, a great many of them died.

She had had such a patient once, a girl of eighteen who looked about ten. The girl simply did not want to grow up. She was beautiful and intelligent, as these people often were, but she could not see what a mess she had become. When she looked in the mirror, so she told Rosemary, she saw a fat woman who needed to slim drastically. What other people saw was a walking skeleton, or very nearly.

It was heartbreaking, and Rosemary eyed Mandy's figure keenly. She had more flesh on her than the patient who had died, but the other signs were there: eyes deep and luminous and much too big for her thin face, clothes arranged casually so that the unobservant wouldn't notice anything amiss, skin that was stretched tautly across her cheekbones, and a deceptively lighthearted, almost happy air. Nothing wrong with me, her demeanour proclaimed. Only the trained eye could see that something was wrong. The trouble was

Rosemary didn't know how far the disease had gone, or even if it *was* anorexia nervosa. Trusting your clinical judgment wasn't always enough.

Craig Dean was right: Sister Miller had problems enough without interfering in Lyn Abbott's private life. Let Craig sort *her* out. It was going to be a very long winter.

Rosemary was on call over the weekend. She wasn't actually required to do any visits but had to be available in case she was needed.

She spent Saturday morning at the surgery, and ended up with a few minor nursing chores. A small boy presented himself with a cut arm, an old lady passing by had a severe nosebleed, then the vicar rang to say that his mother-in-law had collapsed.

The woman must have died only seconds before Dr Tunstall and Rosemary arrived at the Vicarage. Although they tried valiantly to resuscitate her, their efforts were in vain.

Panting, Dr Tunstall glanced up at Rosemary and shook his head. He had been applying the mouth-to-mouth resuscitation while she performed the cardiac compression. The vicar had telephoned for the ambulance, but it wouldn't be needed now. She was an old lady and perhaps it would have been kinder to leave her to die in peace, but one always had to try. Even if they had succeeded, Rosemary felt that too much time had elapsed, and that some brain damage would have occurred. This was another aspect of resuscitation that had to be looked at. It wasn't always as straightforward as the layman seemed to think.

All in all, it was an eventful morning, and she was

glad it was Dr Tunstall on duty. She simply could not face another run-in with Craig Dean.

They had met, briefly, the previous morning, for the usual case conference. Craig had been preoccupied, tense and several times had lost the thread of his conversation. The others had commented on it once he left, and there was speculation that he might be ill.

There was a certain amount of early 'flu about, and SEN Partridge was sure the young doctor was coming down with that.

'He works so hard, poor man. Too hard,' she said in her attractive Sussex burr. Mrs Partridge was a real Sussex countrywoman, a species fast disappearing, and Rosemary had grown fond of her. Now that Gwen had proved to be such a gossip, Rosemary turned more and more to the second-in-command for advice and notes about the patients. Gwen remained helpful, and was a cheerful person to have around, but Rosemary had found out that it was Gwen who had told Craig Dean about the quarrel with Lyn. She suspected she had told Alec about her outing with the doctor, too. It was unfair to blame Lyn for everything.

Rosemary decided to potter around the garden on Saturday afternoon. She half wished she was free and could drive over to see Aunt Lizzie, but that would mean discussing Alec, which her aunt would certainly do at great length.

Sadly, she began to sweep up the fallen leaves. Autumn leaves of red and gold, some dark brown now. Dead, like Alec's love for her. Sighing, she swept the leaves more vigorously, then stopped as she heard the doorbell. Spike, who had been trying to disarrange the leaves, gave his deep-throated bark, and Rosemary hoped whoever it was would be deterred.

She resumed her tidying, then flung the broom down as the bell went again. She hurried to answer the door, belatedly remembering that she was on call. It might be an emergency!

But it wasn't. Instead, a homely, middle-aged woman stood waiting patiently, and Rosemary hugged her. 'Aunt Lizzie! What a lovely surprise!'

She almost dragged her aunt through to the kitchen, knowing she liked nothing better than to sit at the kitchen table, drinking tea and gossiping.

After Rosemary finished tidying the leaves, she and Aunt Lizzie spent the remainder of the afternoon discussing Alec.

Aunt Lizzie, who loved animals, had made an abject slave out of Spike. He lay beside her on the settee, his head resting comfortably on her lap. He had a marked preference for women, Rosemary had noticed. Although reasonably friendly towards Craig Dean, he kept aloof to some extent, and it would be a long time before he grew to trust the doctor completely, she felt. As for his attitude to Alec . . .

She giggled. She could hardly relate the incident about Alec trying to carry her up the stairs and Spike tearing his trousers, but she wished she could!

'I'm sorry, Aunt Lizzie. It was just a passing thought,' she explained, wiping a tear from her eye. 'Spike doesn't take to everyone, and I've had one or two embarrassing incidents,' she added.

Her aunt gave her a sharp look. She had similar

grey eyes to Rosemary's, and there was a faint family resemblance, Aunt Lizzie being her mother's only surviving sister.

'Your mother would have wanted you to be settled,' Aunt Lizzie put in later, when they were having tea. 'Get a nice man and settle down, that's what *our* mother used to say. She didn't hold with being a spinster,' she added sharply, and Rosemary made a noncommittal reply: 'Spinsters are single only because they can't find a good husband.' Aunt Lizzie wasn't to be stopped once she was on her hobby-horse, and Rosemary smiled.

It was useless to tell her that not every girl *wanted* a husband, that nowadays there were more careers open to women. Aunt Lizzie, a widow for several years, believed that a woman's place was in the home, and that marriage was the only career worthy of the name.

'I suppose I've had my own way for so long that I can't bear to be told what to do. I don't *need* a husband,' Rosemary said firmly.

It was true. Men had no place in her future —particularly Craig Dean, who was far too arrogant. She smiled sadly, remembering his words about not being brought to heel.

Even if he did his own washing, he could never be less than masculine, never be other than lovable and . . .

'Rosemary! Whatever is it? Rosemary!' Aunt Lizzie began to shake her, and Spike growled warningly.

Automatically, Rosemary reached out to soothe the dog, her mind far away. 'I'm all right, Aunt Lizzie. Really,' she murmured, staring ahead unseeingly. 'It's just another passing thought.'

'It seems to me you're having a lot of passing thoughts!' her aunt grumbled. 'You've gone all glassy-eyed, just like a woman in love,' she added triumphantly. 'But then you *are* a woman in love. I shall tell Alec so!'

Just like a woman in love. Rosemary put a hand despairingly to her face. She felt hot and cold at the same time. Oh why, *why* hadn't she seen it before? Ecstasy mingled with the sadness, the sheer anguish. She *was* in love, but with Craig Dean!

It was the tall, fair-haired doctor she had been yearning for all week, a man who saw her only as a useful nursing Sister—a man who did not return her love, and never would.

Ecstasy died, and the anguish, the sheer heartache, surfaced. She loved Craig, but she could never have him, they could never belong together. Knowing that, how could she go on, day after day, working with him, nursing his patients, watching him and Lyn together?

The answer was that she could not, but nor could she leave. The old eternal triangle had really caught her! She had wasted all those weeks, yearning over Alec Scott, a man clearly unworthy of *any* woman's love, though she hoped he would one day find happiness. It would not be with her, that was for sure.

Now she was at a crossroads, and simply did not know which way to turn. She so longed to find the signpost marked 'Happiness'!

Yet doctors and nurses could not put their own selfish desires before their duty to the patients. She had contracted to work here, had been absorbed into the practice, and certainly couldn't leave them now. Besides, she didn't want to leave. She liked Hurstfield, and was just beginning to get to know the patients.

She shrugged philosophically, absently patting Spike's soft, wet nose. She must simply grin and bear it—but oh, how hard that would be!

'Rosemary, if you're going to ignore me I might as well go home!' Aunt Lizzie eyed her sternly, but her eyes twinkled.

No doubt she thought Rosemary was daydreaming about Alec. Rosemary smiled fondly at her. No way must she disillusion the poor dear. Craig Dean was unobtainable. Lyn Abbott had *his* future mapped out for him!

Gwen telephoned Rosemary Monday lunchtime to say that the young doctor was ill.

'Came down with this twenty-four-hour 'flu yesterday, or so he says,' Gwen snorted. 'more than likely he was ill on Saturday but wouldn't give in. He'll wear himself to a frazzle, you mark my words!'

Gwen rambled on at some length, but eventually Rosemary managed to get a word in. 'Is there anything I can do, Gwen? Perhaps I could look in on some of the doctor's patients?'

'The old doctor's trying to get round to them,' Gwen assured her. 'He isn't as fit as he was, though. I know Dr Dean wouldn't have gone sick unless he was at death's door,' she added, alarming Rosemary.

Although she couldn't help with any of Dr Dean's patients, Dr Tunstall wanted her to look in on a couple of his, just to reassure them, and Rosemary took down their details from Gwen.

All the while she was writing, her mind was busy. Should she call to see Craig? Most likely Lyn would be there. Naturally she would want to nurse the man she loved. Yet suppose she wasn't there? Suppose Craig was having to cope alone?

'Gwen—about Dr Dean. Is he alone? Can I help out there?' She hated asking Gwen, for inevitably the information would find its way back to Lyn Abbott.

Gwen didn't know who was looking after the doctor, and she didn't know Lyn's precise movements. As far as she knew, Lyn would be reporting for evening surgery as usual.

Still worrying about Craig, Rosemary continued on her round. She was honest enough to admit that *she* wanted to care for Craig Dean, to nurse him until he was well. There was something endearing about a strong man reduced to a state of dependence. Even in sickness, Craig was still strong, virile, yet he needed tender loving care just as the patients did.

Her last patient had a problem for her, a problem she expected to meet in cities but not in the heart of the country: heroin.

In her city work, she had had only a passing acquaintance with drug abuse, yet it was an ever-increasing problem. Somehow, in Hurstfield, it had an alien quality. Surely the village youngsters weren't caught up in a drugs ring?

It was almost a relief to know that the suspected heroin addict, Dave Ritter, was at university.

Mrs Ritter was a colostomy patient. Since the

stoma-care nurse was based in the nearby town and did not often get time to visit the outlying areas, Rosemary had taken on some of her tasks whenever possible.

The specially trained stoma-care nurse visited patients before and after a colostomy operation, advising them on suitable appliances and offering help and encouragement. She also put them in touch with other patients, if requested. Rosemary hadn't time to do all that, but she assisted the special nurse whenever she could.

In Mrs Ritter's case, the colostomy operation had been performed only a couple of months before, and the woman, a widow of fifty, hadn't yet come to terms with the idea of wearing a bag for the rest of her life.

'I feel so unclean, Sister,' she sniffed, as Rosemary gently inspected the stoma itself. 'Then there's this business with Dave. And he was always such a good boy when he was at home.'

Rosemary gave her a cuddle, letting the small but obese women rest her head and sob out her troubles. The wound site was a good colour and there was no offensive odour, and Mrs Ritter had little to worry about there. Her bowel movements had become irregular, and no doubt that worry about her son was affecting the proper working of the colostomy.

'You haven't met my Dave, Sister. He was home for the vacation, but I didn't see a lot of him. Up at the Fairleys' most of the time, he was.'

'Oh? Does he go around with one of the Fairley boys?' asked Rosemary. 'I thought the eldest boy was only sixteen?'

'It's a Fairley *girl*, Sister, that young Mandy. And her not fifteen yet!' Mrs Ritter was clearly shocked.

Rosemary tensed. This could be the key she had been searching for. An unsuitable romance went some way towards explaining Mandy's behaviour. Yet anorexia nervosa patients weren't usually interested in the opposite sex. They didn't *want* to grow up, have normal relations, marry and have babies.

It was all very confusing, and her head ached by the time she left Mrs Ritter. The woman had seen one of the posters they had in the surgery: Skin care by courtesy of heroin. It had worried her so much that it had affected the working of the colostomy and left her depressed and anxious.

There was no concrete evidence that Dave was taking drugs, just a caring mother's suspicions, and Rosemary didn't quite know what she could do to help. In the city there was usually a health visitor who dealt with drug abuse. Then there were back-up facilities that Hurstfield didn't have. The university authorities were the people to approach really, but a vague suspicion wasn't sufficient. Margaret Gearing would be the best person to consult, and she would ask Margaret to call on Mrs Ritter.

Dr Tunstall telephoned her the following evening. It was dusking over and she'd just returned from walking Spike, glad that she *could* walk alone in the evening without the constant fear of being attacked. There was no doubt about it, this rural life was for her.

If only the man she loved returned that love, life in Hurstfield would be idyllic. But life was never like that, she acknowledged with a trace of cynicism. Perhaps in the summer she would see things differently, be more positive. Perhaps, too, the heartache would have lessened by then.

Lyn had, as Rosemary suspected, been looking after Craig. Rosemary had telephoned the Tunstalls earlier and been told that everything was under control, that Craig was being well looked after. He wouldn't let his elderly housekeeper in the house while he was ill, but Lyn was doing her best. Now there was, it appeared, another crisis for Lyn and she had been called away. The Tunstalls needed Rosemary's help.

Rosemary wondered if the practice wouldn't be better off without Lyn, but it wasn't for her to say. What *did* concern her was that Craig Dean had been left alone.

She wouldn't have been human if the knowledge hasn't cheered her considerably. Poor Craig, two nurses fighting over the chance to offer him succour in his hour of need!

She called at the Tunstalls' to pick up a key to Craig's house and collect a nourishing broth Mrs Tunstall had made for her nephew.

This time Rosemary took Spike with her. Craig lived on a quiet estate, right at the top of the hill. It wasn't the house Rosemary had seen so many times and had claimed as suitable for him, or for herself. His home was more secluded, she mused, driving along the tree-lined road.

Each house had a small area of wood at the back, and Craig's had an enormous garden back and front. Of course it was only rented, as he'd said, and she wondered why he hadn't bought one. Was he planning to leave the village? He had said once that he didn't intend to spend the rest of his life in Hurstfield. Once Lyn's problems were solved, if they ever were, they might move away.

It might be easier to bear then. Seeing them together every day would become unbearable.

She could stay in Hurstfield then. She and Spike, growing old together . . .

Craig was downstairs when she cautiously let herself in the front door. He was at the back of the house and that was why she hadn't seen a light.

He looked ghastly, and Rosemary felt like ordering him to bed. If it had been anyone but the strong-willed Craig Dean, she would have done so. As it was, an argument would sap his strength, and perhaps he felt better up.

'Uncle Ernest said he'd sent you, but there was no need, Rosemary,' he said huskily. He was still feverish and it sounded as if the infection had gone to his chest.

'All right, if you don't need me, I'll go!' she said lightly. 'Come on, Spike. Dr Dean doesn't need us!'

'Doesn't he?' Craig said softly. 'I rather think he does.'

Rosemary turned swiftly, her attention caught by something in the tone of his voice.

CHAPTER SEVEN

ROSEMARY decided she must have mistaken the inflection in Craig's voice. When he wanted to be, he could be very charming, and he was probably trying to put her at her ease, ensure that she didn't feel she was in the way.

'I got bored and lonely upstairs, so I've moved down here.' Craig led the way to the study, which was at the back of the house. It was warm and cosy, and he had made himself as comfortable as possible, on a bed which Rosemary considered was far too small for such a big man.

'I think I'll lie down again,' he muttered, passing a hand wearily across his face. He was beginning to need a shave. A lock of damp hair hung limply across his forehead, his eyes were bloodshot, and his serviceable brown dressing-gown had a button missing.

He was more endearing than ever to Rosemary, if he did but know it, and automatically she reached out to help him take off his dressing-gown. Expertly she turned back the bed, then removed his slippers while he sat on the edge of the bed.

Meekly, Craig allowed her to tuck him in and rearrange his pillows so that he could lie down.

'Ah, this is Utopia!' he sighed, as Rosemary made a final adjustment to the covers. He smiled lazily up at her, and her heart filled with love for him.

Briskly she turned away, calling to Spike, who had followed them. 'You need a good rest, doctor. Give me a call when you want some fluids. Your Aunt Annie sent you some chicken broth.'

'Not now, Lyn,' he said drowsily, his eyes already closed. 'Leave me in peace, there's a good girl.'

Pain shot through her, and she despised herself for the hollow feeling his words caused. Already he had forgotten the big, capable Sister Miller. His tired mind was focused on one person—Lyn Abbott.

Feeling extremely sorry for herself, Rosemary settled down in the kitchen, eyeing the beige wall without enthusiasm.

The whole house needed redecorating. As decorating was one of her interests, she spent the next half hour busily planning a colour scheme for the house. The sitting-room was acceptable, and she rather liked the blue and silver striped wallpaper, but everywhere else was so drab. The main bedroom was the only other room with papered walls, but that paper needed replacing.

Yet if the house was only rented, presumably furnished, it wasn't up to Craig Dean to refurbish it. Now, if he bought that house she so much admired, there was no limit to what could be done. They could work on it together . . .

Sighing, she settled in the comfortable old chair, and must have dozed, for she heard Craig calling in the distance, and it took a few seconds for her to rouse herself.

Annoyed at having slept on duty, Rosemary stumbled to the study in her stockinged feet.

Craig was sitting up in bed, staring feverishly about him. 'Lyn? Is that you?' He peered at Rosemary, shielding his eyes from the light in the hall.

Sad that she wasn't the woman he was seeking, she said gently: 'No, I'm Rosemary. I've popped in to see how you are. Lyn isn't here.'

Craig clutched at her arm, and she stumbled and fell against the bed. Spike growled, and she murmured soothing words to him as she struggled to free herself from the doctor's grip of steel. For a sick man, he had plenty of strength.

'Poor Craig.' Rosemary wasn't aware that she had spoken aloud until Craig laughed harshly.

'Poor Craig! Why? What's the matter with me? I'll be all right in a few hours. I . . .' His grip relaxed, and he fell back.

She leaned over him, smoothing back that wayward lock of hair. She wondered briefly if she ought to call Dr Tunstall, but experience had taught her that a good night's sleep worked wonders. Once his temperature dropped, he would be fine. He had been taking Paracetamol, she knew, and she would have liked to get another couple of them into him. He——

Without warning, his hands reached out for her, and she was crushed against his chest. 'Lyn,' he murmured. 'Oh, Lyn, I need you so!'

Before Rosemary could protest, his lips found hers. She responded eagerly, putting into that kiss all the love, all the longing she felt for him. He would never know. If he remembered the kiss when he awoke, he would assume that he had been dreaming. As it was, he believed he held Lyn

Abbott in his arms.

How he could mistake her curvy body for Lyn's angular one was a question Rosemary hardly bothered with. Even though it was under false pretences, she was in Craig's arms, and that was all that mattered.

Spike seemed to have realised that all was well, for he lay down beside the bed, making no move to attack Craig.

Rosemary sighed and snuggled closer to Craig. She wasn't particularly comfortable, half lying, half kneeling by the bed. There certainly wasn't room for her to lie beside him, but she managed somehow, moving stealthily, trying not to disturb the now sleeping man.

Lying there was bitter-sweet, but it was all she could ever hope for from Craig. 'Good night, my darling,' she whispered, knowing he couldn't hear her.

Hours later, she was awakened by Spike's exciting baying. Then the doorbell rang and kept ringing, and reluctantly she got up. Her foot had gone to sleep, and she stumbled and sat down heavily on the floor, wakening Craig.

'All right, I'm coming!' Rosemary called to the inconsiderate person who kept his finger on the bell.

Craig chuckled weakly, and she shot him a concerned glance. He *looked* better. The feverish light was gone from his eyes, and he was cooler, she noted as she pressed her hand professionally against his brow.

She only hoped he remembered nothing of the night. He would probably wonder what she was doing beside his bed, but she could easily explain that away.

Dr Tunstall brushed past her the moment she opened the front door. 'Thought you were both dead!' he boomed. 'I've got better things to do than stand on patients' doorsteps!' he added for good measure, and Rosemary chuckled. He was in good form this morning!

The old doctor was standing frowning down at Craig when Rosemary returned to the study. 'When did he last have his tablets?' he demanded. 'Well? Come on, Sister, I haven't got all day!' Dr Tunstall shot her an accusing look, and she flushed.

'He—I was going to give him some last night, but——'

'But I refused,' Craig put in smoothly. 'I don't like the taste—I've had several doses. Don't fuss, Uncle Ernest, there's a good chap.'

Dr Tunstall spluttered, 'Don't fuss, he says! I send you a trained nurse, a *Sister* no less, and she lets you get away with murder!' he grumbled.

He folded his stethoscope, then stuffed it into his pocket. 'Rest today, Craig, then we'll see about you coming back.'

'What *is* today?' Craig turned puzzled blue eyes on Rosemary, and seemed astonished to learn that it was Wednesday morning. '*Is* it? Whatever happened to Tuesday, I wonder?'

'Yes, I wonder, too,' his uncle said gruffly, giving Rosemary a piercing look from under his bushy brows. Those eyes saw more than was good for her, and she hastened to show him out. The sooner she was alone, the better. Once she had given Craig his breakfast, he could be left.

'Will Lyn be coming over today?' she asked, as they stood on the doorstep.

'Lyn? Couldn't say. Couldn't say, my dear.' His wrath forgotten, Dr Tunstall patted her cheek, bestowed a charming smile on her, then ambled out to his car.

The old man was as hard to fathom as Craig, and Rosemary smiled indulgently as she waved him off. He hadn't mentioned it, but it was likely that his wife would be over some time during the day. They could hardly expect Rosemary to spend a whole working day with Craig.

But that, it appeared, was what they intended. Annie Tunstall telephoned just before lunch to find out whether they had enough to eat. Her husband didn't want her to risk catching whatever bug Craig was suffering from.

'I know you'll take good care of him, Sister!' she trilled, and Rosemary could only assure her that she would spend what remained of the day with their nephew. Mrs Tunstall told her not to worry about the day's nursing duties, that they would be carried out.

Lunch was late, but adequate. Rosemary heated the broth for Craig and cut him a thin slice of bread and butter. She found some dry rice in the cupboard, and there was sufficient milk for a proper rice pudding.

Craig enjoyed her pudding so much that he had two helpings, and Rosemary glowed inwardly. Being allowed to cook an invalid meal for the man she loved was little enough, but it was the only expression of her love she could show.

She saved the rice pudding for Craig, telling him

there would be enough for him the following day. 'That is if Lyn isn't back by then,' she added hesitantly, as she collected his dishes.

He was sitting up in the armchair by now, and had told her he intended to dress later on.

'No, Lyn won't be back for a day or so. Steve is with Lyn's sister over in Hastings, in case you were wondering.' Craig frowned. 'I'm surprised Aunt Annie hasn't been over.'

'She phoned. She was afraid she might catch the plague, I think!' chuckled Rosemary, and Craig raised a brow.

Blue eyes regarded her thoughtfully. 'I imagine my aunt decided you would be more than adequate,' he said softly, and she blushed.

She could almost *hear* the colour rising, and knew her pale face must be glowing. She only hoped he did not realise just how much tender loving care she had given him!

'Doctor never does,' Craig smiled, and Rosemary almost choked.

'I—I beg your pardon?' She fixed a smile to her mouth.

'Doctor never chases blondes. Isn't that what Gwen Sayers has been telling you? She's absolutely right,' he added, before Rosemary could gather her wits.

'I'll leave you to dress, doctor,' she said primly, and his laughter followed her.

Doctor never does. Well, of course he didn't. She knew that without being hit on the head by the fact. Being fair himself, he preferred brunettes. It was only natural.

Sadly, she cast an eye at her reflection in the

mirror. Pale lemon hair, pale grey eyes, pale complexion, too. How insipid she must seem beside the Lyn Abbotts of this world!

Once Craig was showered and dressed, Rosemary made him sit by the fire in the sitting room. Despite his weak protests, she got him to take two Paracetamol and, later, a lemon drink to ease his aching throat.

'I hope you aren't thinking of going back to work tomorrow,' she ventured, as all three of them sat by the fire that evening. 'Another day off would do you the world of good,' she added, casting an anxious eye in his direction.

'So it would,' Craig agreed, 'but I can't leave Uncle Ernest to cope alone. He isn't getting any younger.'

Rosemary didn't think Dr Tunstall would mind coping for another day, but she knew Craig would be back on duty within a few hours.

'Don't fret, Rosemary. I'm tougher than I look.' Craig's tone was gentle, and she glanced up at him. They were sitting side by side, with Spike lying across her feet.

'I wasn't fretting. Your health is your own concern, Craig,' she said pointedly. She made a show of glancing at the clock. 'I really have to be getting home. Duty calls tomorrow.'

She rose, determined to make her leavetaking as brief as possible. Craig might want to telephone Lyn, and he must be wondering how she was getting on. Rosemary wondered herself. She couldn't imagine who had called the woman away, and assumed it was legal business over the divorce.

Craig let her out, and to her surprise Spike allowed the doctor to stroke him.

'Thank you for all your help, Rosemary,' Craig said quietly as they stood in the hall. He seemed about to say more, then abruptly his lips tightened, and Rosemary wondered at that.

Their eyes met and held, then she glanced away, wishing she looked rather more elegant. Her fawn slacks had seen better days, and the sweater wasn't new. She had tied her long hair back casually with a piece of blue ribbon, and she saw Craig's eyes stray to it. She thought he was contrasting her appearance with that of the fastidiously neat Lyn Abbott. Inevitably, Sister Miller would come off worse.

'I hope Lyn comes back soon,' she said impulsively. Then to her own amazement, and probably his as well, she stood on tiptoe and kissed Craig's brow. 'Take care,' she whispered, shooing Spike out of the door and following him quickly.

What, she wondered as she drove away, had possessed her? How could she kiss him like that? Her concentration wavered, and the car moved erratically. Silently cursing *all* men, she drove more carefully.

True, she had kissed his brow, not his lips, but even so . . . It was hardly professional, and must never happen again.

But then the opportunity for such a close relationship with Craig would not happen again. He was well on the road to recovery—and Lyn would soon be back.

The next few days and the weekend passed uneventfully. Rosemary went to visit Mrs Fairley early the following week. She brought Mandy casually into the conversation, without mentioning the suspected slimmers' disease.

It was Mrs Fairley herself who brought up the subject of her daughter's poor appetite. 'She's getting that thin, Sister! Hardly eats enough to keep body and soul together.'

'Teenagers often go through phases like that,' Rosemary assured her. 'They believe they're getting fat, so they diet over-strenuously. Has she any particular friends?' she asked, wondering if Mrs Fairley knew about Dave Ritter. 'Sometimes if one girl diets, they all follow suit.'

Mrs Fairley snorted, 'You're right there, Sister! Like a lot of sheep, they are. My Mandy hasn't got a close friend, now you come to mention it. She used to bring one or two girls home from school, but not recently.'

'No boy-friends yet, I suppose?' Rosemary threw in casually.

'No! Well, that Ritter boy used to hang around, but my husband saw *him* off! He's far too old for Mandy. He's at the university now,' Mrs Fairley explained, and Rosemary was careful to express her surprise.

When she left, she was no nearer a solution to the problem of Mandy Fairley. She decided she would await any further developments.

Lyn Abbott returned to work at the beginning of the week, and Rosemary was careful not to make any personal comments. They exchanged a civil 'good morning', but that was all.

Craig was back in the swing of things, though Rosemary knew from experience how the after-effects of 'flu hung on, sometimes for weeks. He seemed to be suffering from the lassitude, the inertia which often followed, and she noticed that his rounds were taking longer now.

Gwen Sayers commented on it, as might be expected, and also complained that Lyn wasn't pulling her weight. 'I'm having to do everything, Sister,' she moaned. 'That Lyn Abbott is supposed to do four evenings, but she's only done two this week. And I'm that busy, I don't know where to turn!'

Rosemary gave a noncommittal smile. 'I'm that busy as well, Gwen. What with 'flu and a few mild cases of whooping cough.'

'It'll get worse afore it gets better,' Gwen said darkly.

Probably Gwen didn't mean her remark to be depressing, but it left Rosemary feeling low. That was the danger time for infections. They attacked when the body's defences were depressed and off guard, and she simply hadn't time to catch 'flu.

It was cold and damp the next day, but it was Friday. Rosemary had the weekend off to look forward to, but when there was no one to share the weekend, it seemed pointless to take the time off. She thought she might visit Mrs Fairley on the Saturday morning. She would catch Mandy at home then.

No more had been said about Dave and his drug-taking, but when he came home for the Christmas vacation, Rosemary had promised to see him. What she could do, she didn't know, but universities were active breeding grounds for drug-pushers, and even the most intelligent of teenagers were vulnerable. Unfortunately, drug-takers often encouraged their girl- or boy-friends to join them, and Rosemary thought about Mandy Fairley.

She was sighing over the problem as she prepared to leave that morning. Unusually, she had two patients who were to be bathed. Normally, baths were done by the auxiliaries or Mrs Partridge. It was no longer the practice for a district nursing Sister to perform tasks which could equally well be carried out by auxiliaries.

One auxiliary was on leave, and another was away with 'flu, so Rosemary was glad to chip in and help out. It meant she had less time for brooding, anyway.

Of course she thought about Craig constantly. Often she imagined him and Lyn together. She wondered what they talked about, how many of Lyn's problems Craig was expected to solve, what they did when they weren't locked in each other's arms . . .

Craig was brilliant—it hadn't taken her long to discover that. Some GPs were merely mediocre, but he could have had a career as an outstanding specialist, perhaps in the field of cardiac medicine, since he appeared to enjoy that side most.

Lyn Abbott was, Rosemary considered, merely run-of-the-mill. Craig needed someone more intellectual, a partner who could match him in more ways than Lyn could.

Of course Rosemary knew she was being arrogant in assuming that *she* was his equal. Yet she knew she would be a better wife for him than Lyn.

Lyn was prettier, though. Slender and elegant,

too. Men took account of those things; they weren't interested in a girl's brain.

Feeling extremely hard done by, Rosemary was about to get into her car, when the man in question drove up.

He smiled as she went over to his car. Because she must hide her love, Rosemary became brisk and efficient, filling him in on various patients.

Because they were all behind with their work, there was to be no case-conference this morning, and she assumed that was why he had stopped by the cottage.

'It's such a depressing day that I thought I'd cheer myself up and dine out tonight,' said Craig, with that charming smile he could turn on at will.

'Oh? I hope you have an enjoyable dinner,' Rosemary told him. She wished he hadn't told her. She didn't *want* to know that he was wining and dining Lyn Abbott tonight, though she could spend *her* evening working out where they might go, what they might eat, what they would say to each other. She had got to the stage where every little item about the loved one was carefully stored away, locked in her memory and taken out at intervals and pored over.

She had something more tangible, too. She had found out that he had written a number of articles, both for the GP magazine and the more learned press. Copies of some of his articles now rested safely in her dressing-table drawer.

'Penny for them, Rosemary,' he said gently, and she coloured.

'Oh, it was nothing. Really.' Her tone was un-convincing, and Craig probably imagined she was daydreaming about Alec, but it was of no interest to him, anyway. Nothing she thought or did or said was of any interest to Craig, unless it affected the patients in some way.

His lips tightened. 'If it was nothing, it's hardly worth thinking about, Rosemary. Forget him, for God's sake!' he snapped, blue eyes stormy.

They turned darker, almost grey, when he was angry, and Rosemary paused, unable to tear her gaze away. The ache was almost physical, and it frightened her. She wanted to spend the rest of her life gazing into those eyes, running her fingers through his fair hair, ministering to his every need. She wanted to love and cherish him as long as they both lived, in sickness as well as in health . . . And oh, how it hurt that she could not!

If she admitted that she had almost forgotten Alec, Craig would wonder what was making her so sad—wonder, too, what man she was daydreaming about. Better he did not know. She smiled bravely. 'I can't forget. Could *you* forget someone you once thought you loved?'

Craig shrugged, the storm abating as quickly as it had risen. 'How about dinner, then?'

'Dinner?' she echoed. 'You told me you were dining out with—with . . .' Her voice trailed away. He hadn't exactly *said* he was taking Lyn out to dinner, but he had allowed her to assume it.

He read her thoughts correctly. 'I said I was dining out to cheer myself up. I want *you* to come out with me. Will you, Rosemary? Please?'

Rosemary hated herself for her weakness in accepting, but of course there was no question of turning him down. Dinner with Craig Dean! She was a lucky girl, even if he was offering her only crumbs when she would have liked the whole cake!

They dined at an elegant, old-fashioned inn just outside London. It was largely eighteenth-century, but the bar area went back to the late sixteenth century, the time of William Shakespeare.

'It's quite likely that Shakespeare knew this inn,' said Craig with a smile, as they sat on plush stools at the bar.

It was cosy and intimate, and Rosemary breathed in the olde-worlde atmosphere. She could well believe that Shakespeare had sat in the original tavern drinking ale, and perhaps even slept there. Most of the older building had long gone, but she could almost see the Elizabethan bucks gathering about the huge log fire. It spluttered and hissed merrily while they drank, and she basked in its warmth.

'I'm a sun-worshipper,' she admitted. 'Right now I could do with an autumn holiday. Somewhere with blue skies and an even bluer sea.'

'A tropical isle, perhaps?'

Rosemary nodded. 'Mm. The Bahamas would be nice, or——'

'You'd soon get bored, Rosemary.' Craig spoke decisively. 'Like me, you need to be stretched intellectually. Lotus-eating isn't for you, even for a week. You know you'd miss the patients!' he added lightly. 'Come on, our table is ready.' Steely fingers settled under her elbow, and she was propelled gently but firmly into the more modern part which housed the restaurant.

Theirs was the best table in the restaurant, she decided, casting her eye over the others. They were by the window, which overlooked the river. As the evening was so damp, they wouldn't be able to stroll by the river, but that was a pleasure to be saved for another evening.

Then she remembered, and her face fell. For them, there would not be another evening. Craig must want to talk shop tonight, or was merely lonely. There could be no other reason for taking her out—could there?

A little flame of hope kindled within her, and she chose her meal with renewed hope. What if Craig *was* falling for her, had brought her out tonight to get to know her better? What if . . .

Smiling wryly, she glanced up from the menu.

Craig's blue eyes were smiling over at her, and all thoughts of food vanished from her mind.

CHAPTER EIGHT

'THANK YOU for your company, Rosemary,' Craig said softly, and she dropped her gaze to the menu.

'It's my pleasure,' she smiled. 'It isn't often I get wined and dined.'

'Poor Rosemary! Do you miss him that much?'

Startled, she blurted out: 'Miss who? Oh, you mean Alec! Yes, naturally, I miss him.'

Annoyed with herself for forgetting that she was supposed to be pining, she concentrated on the menu. 'I—I'll have the roast chicken, I think,' she said, without glancing up. She pretended to consider the important question of the starter. 'Everything looks good, Craig. I really don't know what to choose.'

'Lyn likes me to choose for her, but you surprise me, Rosemary. You're always so decisive, so sure,' Craig said, with a little smile.

'No, I'm not!' she cried. Mindful of the waiter's presence, she subsided, his words rankling. 'I'll have the mushroom soup, thank you.'

'The soup it is,' he agreed gently. He ordered the same for himself, then eyed Rosemary thoughtfully.

'Did I insult you by suggesting you were decisive?' he asked, once the soup arrived.

She gazed down at her bowl. 'It made me sound rather masculine,' she said evasively. 'Contrasting me with Lyn wasn't entirely fair. She's always had someone to carry her burdens. I haven't. Alec used to try.' She smiled reminiscently. 'He said he liked my self-assurance, my independent manner, but maybe he hoped I would change, become the sweet, simpering type of girl he's used to.'

'All beauty and no brains? No, Rosemary, I'm sure he liked you for what you are, just as I do. I admire your decisiveness,' Craig assured her.

'Do you?' Surprised, Rosemary met his gaze at last. 'I thought men liked to be boss, make all the decisions. Keep the little woman firmly under the thumb!' she added, with a smile.

He frowned, and she wondered what she had said to upset him. 'That's in emotional relationships. Rosemary. Here, between us, it's good that you're positive, mature. It's essential that I can rely on you in an emergency.'

'I hope you can.' Disappointed beyond belief, she concentrated on the food. All he wanted was for Sister Miller to be positive and reliable in an emergency. He didn't want her as a woman, he didn't even *see* her as a woman! If he had a robot to do her work, he would be just as satisfied.

At any other time, Rosemary would have enjoyed the chicken. Craig's words had killed her appetite, though, and she merely made a token gesture towards the food.

He did not share her lack of appetite, nor did he appear to notice her quietness. 'Tell me about the article,' he said suddenly, and she started.

'Article? What article?' Surely he didn't know about the copies in her dressing-table drawer?

'You've turned an interesting shade of pink,' Craig commented, raising a brow. 'Did you think you could hide your achievements?'

'Achievements? I—Oh! You mean *my* article!' Her face cleared. Craig meant the one and only article she had written. He didn't know about her squirrel-like determination to collect everything he ever wrote!

'My uncle told me you did some research on the inner-city riots, and possible solutions,' he added.

'Yes, I did. I can't imagine why you should be interested, Craig,' Rosemary said bluntly.

'I admire your abilities. I told you, I can't stand stupid women.' He leaned forward, and she almost did the same.

Pulling herself together, she briefly sketched the article, pointing out that she had no foolproof solutions to the problem of inner-city deprivation. 'But if only you could see them, Craig!' As always when discussing her work and patients, her face became animated, her eyes alive with enthusiasm. 'When all hope has gone, what is there? Only a grey void,' she finished.

It was true. When she contrasted her former patients with those in Hurstfield, she could have cried. Here in Sussex, although there was poverty and a certain amount of unemployment, at least there was still hope.

She encouraged Craig to talk about his own articles, and a paper he was to read to a group of senior consultants at the local hospital. His main interest, apart from heart conditions, was preventive medicine.

'That's where *you* come in, Rosemary,' he said gently, and Rosemary nodded dutifully.

Of course. Another task for the decisive Sister

Miller. Preventive medicine *was* important, but was all too often pushed to one side. Money could stretch only so far. She had helped set up such a clinic in her previous post, and now Craig planned a similar clinic.

Helping to get the clinic on its feet was one way of showing her love for him. Some women cooked, cleaned, ironed shirts as an expression of their love for a man. She had no right to do that, but she would express her love for him in the only way she could—by her care and consideration for his patients, and by helping to set up whatever project he wanted.

Nothing definite was to be done about the preventive medicine clinic until early the following spring. They could not spare the time or the resources until any winter epidemics were over. The expected onsurge of whooping cough cases was particularly worrying, and she and Craig discussed the matter during the long drive home.

It was pleasant sitting in the big, comfortable car next to the man she loved, and Rosemary closed her eyes and relaxed as she listened to Craig. Childhood ailments wasn't a romantic subject, true, but talking shop was all they had in common, and any contact with him was welcome, however brief.

Some time during the discussion she must have dozed, for the next thing she remembered was Craig shaking her gently.

'Wake up, sleepytown gal! We're home!'

Rosemary sat up, horrified to think she'd slept when she could have been listening to Craig. Whatever would he think?

He wasn't cross, if his tender expression was anything to go by. 'Did I bore you?'

Rosemary began to protest. Boring was the last thing Craig Dean was, but she couldn't protest *too* vehemently. 'I'm so dreadfully sorry, Craig! It must be the dreary weather. I——'

He silenced her with a kiss. When they drew apart, she had temporarily lost the power of speech, the power of thought, too.

Craig's breathing was ragged, uneven, and she dared to hope that he cared a little. If the kiss meant even a little to him, she would be satisfied.

He saw her into the cottage, switched on all the lights, made a fuss of Spike, then left, after refusing coffee.

Rosemary made her evening cocoa after she had fed Spike. He whined to go out, and she let him into the rear garden. Stroking his rough fur, she gazed unseeingly out into the night. The drizzle had ceased, but it was cold now, the nights hinting of winter to come. The end of October, the fall of the leaf.

It was, she felt, a depressing time of year for those whose love was unrequited. She loved Craig with all her heart. This searing flame was trying to tear her body apart, and she didn't know how much longer she could keep it a secret.

There was only one antidote—work, work and yet more work. Sighing, she closed out the pitch-black night, and bent to wipe Spike's paws. The beautiful dress she'd worn lay across the back of a chair. It was a deep rose-pink, with a softly flared skirt and a bodice which accentuated her full breasts. She had bought it before moving down to the Forest, and tonight was the first time it had come out of the wardrobe.

Cinderella's ball-gown. Now it was after midnight, and Cinderella' pretty dress had turned back into rags.

With a wry smile, she settled down beside the fire with the *Nursing Times*. There was an article on immunisation she ought to read. Back to the grindstone, Sister Miller!

After a busy and fruitful weekend, Rosemary was eager to return to duty on Monday morning. Whatever dark thoughts a late autumn Monday morning brought, she could cope, knowing that some time during the day she might see Craig Dean.

Craig's morning surgery was full, but Rosemary managed to see him before he started.

She was a striking figure in her dark blue Sister's uniform, silver belt buckle holding the navy petersham belt around her neat waist. She had a better figure than she knew, and there were many admiring glances from the patients as her tall, proud figure disappeared through the doctor's door.

Craig glanced up, eyes bleak, and Rosemary's euphoria vanished in a puff of smoke. She managed to smile at him. 'Typical Monday morning, is it?'

He gave a rueful smile, and she liked the way his eyes lit up. The faint lines at the corners of his eyes deepened, and she had the absurd desire to smooth away those lines, to cradle his face in her hands, and kiss away all his cares.

Since she could not, she gave him instead a

crisp, matter-of-fact report on Mrs Fairley, and mentioned young Mandy.

'There isn't much more you can do about Mandy,' Craig assured her. 'Coming right out with your suspicions could prove negative—the girl will simply retreat. I'd adopt a policy of "wait and see" a little longer.'

He passed a hand wearily across his eyes, then reached into his drawer for some tablets. They were Paracetamol, Rosemary saw, and he chuckled at her anxious gaze.

'I'm not addicted to them, Rosemary, don't worry. I've got one hell of a headache—probably the after-effects of the 'flu.'

Rosemary tut-tutted at him. 'You don't take proper care of yourself, Dr Dean! You need plenty of fluids, regular meals . . .' She began to tick the items off on her long, slim fingers, and Craig crumpled up his sheet of blotting paper and threw it playfully at her.

Hastily, she stiffled the giggle which arose. She bent over to pick up the blotting paper, then there was a perfunctory tap at the door, and Lyn Abbott entered.

Lyn's suspicious gaze went from Rosemary's crouched figure to Craig's, and Rosemary withdrew hastily. The smile she gave Lyn wasn't returned, and she was glad to get away from the woman. Let Craig cope with her.

She met Mrs Honeysett the younger while she was on her rounds the next day. After that initial visit to the surgery, Rosemary had seen little of her. She had handed the case over to the SEN. Mrs Honeysett and Nurse Partridge had known each other for years, and it seemed the best course at the time.

Now Mrs Honeysett felt she might need to see a gynaecologist. 'I get that embarrassed, Sister,' she explained, 'and I don't want to bother Dr Dean again. Can't you get me referred?'

That, as Rosemary explained, was something she couldn't do. 'You have to be referred by your own doctor, Mrs Honeysett. It's up to him to decide whether you need to see a specialist. It's probably something he can treat himself. You've had pessaries before for the discharge, haven't you?'

Mrs Honeysett nodded. 'Will you come in with me, Sister? I don't want to go alone. Not at evening surgery, anyway,' she added.

Rosemary knew she was thinking of Lyn Abbott, whom she disliked. Taking the woman to evening surgery was more convenient, though, and if she explained the situation to Craig, he might see them at the beginning of the surgery.

Rosemary and Mrs Honeysett duly presented themselves that evening. A lunchtime telephone call to Craig had ensured that he would see them first. But unfortunately, the moment Lyn set eyes on Mrs Honeysett, she started to argue with the patient. It didn't help matters that Mrs Honeysett gave as good as she got, and Granny Cole was mentioned several times, the patient accusing Lyn of neglecting the old woman. Of course that was true, but it was a subject better not mentioned, as Rosemary knew to her cost.

They were there before the patients, so the only people who heard the argument were Rosemary and Craig Dean himself.

Taking a deep breath, Rosemary tried to part the women, attempting to divert her patient by telling her that Dr Dean would be waiting.

'I'm not ready yet,' Mrs Honeysett said stubbornly. 'This young madam has a few home truths coming to her, and this is as good a time as any to tell her!'

Rosemary began firmly to propel Mrs Honeysett towards Craig's consulting room, but he appeared before she had made any headway.

'I don't think this *is* a good time to tell Mrs Abbott what you think of her,' he said sharply, standing aside so that the two women could precede him into the room.

The expression on his face was ominous, and Rosemary knew she would get the lion's share of the blame for the altercation.

She could hear Lyn crying as she closed the door on her. They weren't the stifled sobs that anyone else might make; she was crying loudly, rather as a child might. Rosemary couldn't help feeling sorry for her. That was part of the trouble. How could you dislike someone for whom you felt pity? The Lyn Abbotts of this world needed help, and Rosemary knew she wasn't qualified to help.

Craig called her back after she had seen Mrs Honeysett off the premises. Lyn was sitting in the reception office once again, but Rosemary didn't go in. The waiting room was full by now, and she exchanged a few words with those patients she knew, before obeying the summons she dreaded.

Craig kept his voice down, but his stony expression caused her heart to skip a beat. Why, she wondered, was *she* always the whipping-boy for Lyn's troubles?

'Why must you keep upsetting Lyn?' Craig began. He rose and began pacing the tiny consulting room.

She watched him, her eyes dark with sorrow. Since she hadn't upset Lyn, she did not intend to answer Craig.

He whirled round, and she flinched at the look in his eyes. 'Well? For God's sake, Rosemary, say something! Lyn is weak and vulnerable,' he went on, before Rosemary could think of anything to say. 'She isn't strong like us. She needs plenty of TLC. That's where *you* come in, Rosemary.'

'At least I'm not Sister Miller at the moment,' she said lightly. 'If I'm still "Rosemary", there's some hope for me.'

A bleak smile crossed the hard features, and her heart swelled with love for him. Why, oh, why couldn't he see that Lyn was stringing him along? Lyn was no more weak and vulnerable than Rosemary herself. She simply used people, and Rosemary found herself telling him so.

He merely shrugged away her words. 'Lyn hasn't been well since Steve was born. She suffered puerperal depression then, and I've been trying to hold her together ever since. It isn't easy, Rosemary. She could crumble any minute. Think of Steve—put *his* needs first, if you really can't spare any sympathy for Lyn.'

Feeling horribly selfish and wicked, Rosemary agreed to put Steve's needs first.

They parted good friends again, and her mouth curved into a smile when Craig told her how much he had enjoyed their evening out.

'So did I, doctor,' she said demurely, and he laughed. 'The meal was superb,' she assured him, then added rashly: 'The kiss was even better!'

She hurried out, before he could comment.

Later that week, Rosemary managed to track down Mandy Fairley. Because of the epidemic, Rosemary tried to make as many calls as she could on patients who had young children or grandchildren, and it was early evening before she drove to the farm. She'd stopped off at her cottage to snatch a cup of tea, having refused to stop for one before. Spike needed a short run, and she was glad of a chance to sit quietly for a few minutes.

Mrs Fairley, Mandy and the two younger children were alone in the house when Rosemary arrived. She duly inspected the leg ulcer, which was almost healed, then chatted generally for a few minutes.

Maddy was restless, replying only in monosyllables when spoken to directly, and Mrs Fairley cast Rosemary a despairing look when Mandy began one of her perambulations across the spacious sitting room.

Rosemary invited the girl to see her off, and Mandy gave her a surprised glance, but did as she was bid.

Once outside, Rosemary hesitated. Being by nature a direct soul, she was at a loss to know how to approach this particular problem. Plunging in might do more harm than good, yet it was a problem she wanted to sort out before winter, if she could.

'How are you keeping, Mandy? I thought you looked a bit peaky,' she began, with a warm smile to let the girl see that she was interested, invite her confidences.

Mandy eyed her suspiciously. 'I'm *sick* of school. I expect that's why I look ill,' she muttered. 'We're off for a whole week now, though,' she volunteered, and Rosemary realised that the coming week was half-term. That gave her an idea.

Knowing that all the Fairleys liked animals, she asked Mandy to help with Spike during the week. 'Unless you've loads of exciting plans?' she added, her gaze watchful.

'Huh! What sort of exciting plans is there in *this* dull old village?' Mandy exploded. 'There's nothing to do, no disco except the Young Farmers'. All there is for us teenagers is TV, or help on the farm, or *Guides*!'

Evidently the Girl Guide movement wasn't Mandy's idea of fun, but neither was anything else, it seemed. The idea of taking Spike for walks was as dull as everything else in Mandy's eyes, and a harassed Rosemary was glad to drive away.

One more failure for that busybody Sister Miller! she mused ruefully. Sometimes she wondered why she bothered.

To Rosemary's great surprise, Mandy turned up at the cottage on Sunday morning, in the company of a tall, very thin youth.

The young lad was Dave Ritter, and Rosemary took to him. He wasn't at all what she had expected, having built up in her mind a picture of a brash youth with long hair and tattoos all over! Dave did have long curls and a rather droppy moustache, but she couldn't see any tattoos and he was a quiet, studious-looking boy. The facial hair, Rosemary suspected, was to cover the acne with which he was liberally covered. Shaving in such circumstances would be painful, anyway. She wondered, briefly, if any part of his skin condition was due to drugs, but she could work round to that subject another time.

Mandy obviously adored him, causing Rosemary to doubt her earlier diagnosis of anorexia nervosa.

They were both willing to take Spike for a walk, and Rosemary sighed, watching the teenage couple disappear into the distance, with the dog. How nice to be young and in love, with no real problems!

Then she remembered the acne, the moral dangers of university life, and the parental resistance. Perhaps being Romeo and Juliet wasn't all fun, after all. At least no one had the right to tell Sister Miller that she couldn't love Dr Dean. Except Lyn, of course.

The pain returned, gnawing away at her like pangs of hunger, only more intense. It was getting to be a permanent ache, and there was no painkiller that could cure love. Her position wasn't so very far from Mandy and Dave's, after all.

During the week, Rosemary saw Mandy Fairley several times. Dave had to return to university, and Mandy was at a loose end.

When Rosemary invited her to tea one evening, the girl made only a token gesture towards the food. Rosemary had taken pains over the meal, too. Being always on the go, she had a healthy appetite usually, and it worried her to see such a big girl eat so little. Although thin, Mandy was as tall as Rosemary herself, but must have weighed several stone less.

She tried not to mention food because she didn't want to frighten the girl away. Yet time was running out.

Early on Friday morning, Rosemary unwittingly walked in on a love scene at the surgery. She had a busy day ahead of her, so she arrived at the surgery early, intending to leave a note on Craig's desk. She had decided that, for once, she would skip the weekly meeting. If there was anything special Craig wanted to tell her, he could always give her a ring. She'd seen Nurse Partridge, and together they had planned next week's work.

Craig, too, was busy, and she hadn't seen him all week. That was more of a disappointment than Rosemary cared to admit. He might at least have called to talk shop, if nothing else.

The object of her thoughts was locked in what appeared to be a passionate embrace with Lyn, and Rosemary blinked in surprise. She hadn't expected to see Craig in so early, and knocking on the door had been a purely reflex action.

Craig glanced up, his arm about Lyn's shoulders. She was grasping his hand, holding on to it for dear life, and as she turned towards Rosemary, there was unmistakable triumph in those pale eyes.

If it hadn't been a silly idea, Rosemary would have believed the tableau was solely for her benefit. Yet the kiss that followed was, she didn't doubt that.

Apparently it took Craig by surprise too, as Lyn

flung her arms about his neck, pulling his head down to her level.

Rosemary, flustered and upset, retreated quickly, closing the consulting room door with a snap behind her. That was that. She couldn't have asked for any clearer proof. Craig and Lyn were in love, and Sister Miller had no business daydreaming, living in a world of what might have been.

Reluctantly, she went to evening surgery. She had one or two matters to discuss with Dr Tunstall, and he had surprised her by inviting her to supper. When she had haltingly tried to make excuses, the old doctor had beamed at her, then patted her on the back.

It was all settled. She was to turn up about seven-thirty or eight. Dr Tunstall hadn't, Rosemary realised, listened to one word of her excuses. An invitation to supper was a Royal command, and that was that!

Since Dr Tunstall had said she could bring Spike, she really had no valid excuse to make. Yet she feared that Craig would also be a guest, and after the scene that morning, she didn't know how she would greet him. He must have been as embarrassed as she was. Then, too, Lyn might be a guest of the Tunstalls.

The heartache of seeing Lyn and Craig together, and perhaps of hearing their wedding plans, would be more than she could bear.

Dwelling on the evening meal to come, Rosemary bumped into Craig before she was even aware of his presence. He paused in the doorway of his consulting room, blue eyes watchful.

Rosemary summoned up a smile. 'Good

evening, Doctor. I was hoping for a few words with Dr Tunstall. He——'

'Have you seen Lyn?' demanded Craig, and, bewildered, Rosemary shook her head. 'She ought to be in the office,' he muttered, brushing past her.

Wherever Lyn was, it wasn't in the office, for Rosemary had noticed several patients waiting at the hatch for attention. It really was too bad of her. She always let poor Craig down, and certainly did not deserve the love of a good man.

Knowing that she was probably being unfair, Rosemary went in search of Dr Tunstall. His consulting room was right at the back, near to the private part of the house, and it was there that Rosemary found Lyn.

She was deep in conversation with a tall, rather swarthy-looking man. His resemblance to Steve was so marked that Rosemary realised he must be the boy's father.

Murmuring an apology, she took a more circuitous route to the old doctor's room. The couple had looked happy enough. Perhaps the tug-of-war over the boy was settled, and the divorce was going ahead smoothly.

It couldn't be that Lyn and her husband had decided to make a fresh start. Could it? For one glorious moment, Rosemary believed the two of them *were* planning to give their marriage another try—then Craig would be free.

Craig was waiting for her when she came out of Dr Tunstall's room. A quick glance around assured her that Lyn and her husband had gone.

Putting on a bright, professional smile for Craig, she apologised for not attending the morning conference. 'That is why I—why I went to your room, to leave a message. I left it with Gwen instead,' she blundered on.

A faint smile lifted the corners of his mouth, and Rosemary wanted to press her lips against his, transfer that shadow of a smile to her own mouth.

'Did you see that man with Lyn?' asked Craig.

She nodded. 'I suppose that was her husband? Is—is everything all right there?' She licked her dry lips and waited, longing for Craig to tell her that Lyn no longer wanted a divorce.

CHAPTER NINE

CRAIG's smile broadened. 'Yes, everything's fine, Rosemary. He——'

Rosemary turned at a slight sound. Lyn was watching them, a satisfied smile on her face. Before Craig could finish his sentence, she came forward and rested her small hand on his arm.

There was no mistaking that proprietorial gesture, nor the tenderness in Craig's eyes as he gazed down at his loved one. So far as Craig was concerned, everything *was* fine. Lyn and her husband had agreed on an amicable divorce—that must have been what he was about to say.

Rosemary didn't wait to hear any more. With a murmured apology, she hurried by, her rubber-heeled shoes squeaking on the tiled floor. Everything's fine, Rosemary. His words echoed and re-echoed in her head as she reached the sanctuary of her car.

She was about to start the engine when Craig called out to her. Reluctantly she wound down the window, hoping he wasn't going to tell her about his wedding plans.

'See you at supper, Rosemary—Aunt Annie said you were coming. We must talk.' His tone brooked no argument.

She swallowed the lump that came into her throat. How she wished she had the courage to turn down the invitation! But Dr Tunstall would not, she knew, allow her to do that, and she didn't want an argument. She would go to supper and hear whatever Craig wanted to tell her.

He frowned as she continued to wrestle silently with her thoughts. 'Is anything the matter, Rosemary?' His voice was tender, concerned.

'No, it's nothing really,' she hedged, avoiding his searching gaze. If she once glanced at him, he would see the misery in her soft grey eyes, and then he would realise how badly she had fallen for him. She had too much pride to ever admit her love.

Craig leaned in at the window, both hands on the window-frame. 'Rosemary, look at me.'

His tone was commanding, and she could not ignore it. They exchanged glances, Rosemary trying desperately to hide the longing she felt.

Craig's eyes narrowed. 'Rosemary——' he began, but she could not bear to hear whatever news he had to tell her.

'Goodbye, Craig,' she said firmly, her composure fast beginning to crumble.

He stepped back from the car, his gaze cool. 'Don't let me keep you,' he said tightly, and Rosemary swallowed the words of love that rose to her lips. There was nothing she could say to him without revealing her secret.

Supper at the Tunstalls was a disaster, though it started well enough. Rosemary was the first to arrive, though Craig was expected shortly.

'He's full of plans for the future!' Annie Tunstall trilled.

Rosemary made a noncommittal reply, and Mrs Tunstall glanced at her sharply. 'His plans concern *you*, Rosemary,' she added, before bustling away to see how the meal was progressing.

Since Dr Tunstall was out on a call, Rosemary was alone in the big, comfortable sitting room, and there was no need to hide the heartache. Craig's plans *did* concern her, in some measure. If he married Lyn Abbott, she felt she could not bear to stay, but that wasn't what his aunt had meant. She must have been speaking of the preventive medicine clinic that Craig hoped to start in the spring. Rosemary would be expected to assist in getting the project under way, for he had said as much.

It was something to look forward to. The only bright spot in an otherwise bleak future, Rosemary felt.

Craig arrived late, after Dr Tunstall, and she made sure she was deep in conversation with the older doctor when she heard Craig's voice.

He helped himself to a whisky, then came over to the huge corner-piece settee where Rosemary sat with his uncle. Immediately she rose, muttering that she ought to see if Mrs Tunstall needed help in the kitchen.

With an exasperated sigh, Craig followed her. 'Look, Rosemary, we have to talk. There's something I——'

'Later, Craig.' Her tone was equally firm. They were in the hallway now, and could be overheard by both the Tunstalls.

'Later be damned!' Before she could take evasive action, Craig pinned her against the wall. Although she was strong, his strength was superior, and she couldn't escape.

Desperate events demanded desperate measures, and Alec's name popped into her head. She grasped at it eagerly, knowing it was the one thing that would stop Craig telling her about poor, poor Lyn ad nauseam.

He did not, it appeared, intend talking at all, for his mouth hovered tantalisingly above hers, and she felt waves of longing wash over her.

'Rosemary.' His voice was husky, and her lips parted in anticipation.

Then Mrs Tunstall called from the kitchen, and Craig's grip relaxed.

'I—I'd better go. Your aunt will need help.' Rosemary cleared her throat, wondering if the lump in her throat was psychological or the beginning of 'flu. Right then, she would have welcomed the 'flu. Fighting that would take her mind off Craig and Lyn.

'I wish I understood you, Rosemary.' Craig sounded exasperated, and her temper rose.

'Well, I understand *you* perfectly, Dr Dean!' Fearing to say too much, she broke free and marched into the kitchen.

How dared he propose to Lyn, then make a pass at *her*!

Remembering Alec, Rosemary brought him into the conversation at the first possible moment. Although Dr Tunstall had modestly called the meal 'supper', it was more of a dinner, and there were three courses.

Melon began the meal, and apart from some desultory conversation between the men, there was silence. Once or twice Rosemary felt Mrs Tunstall's eyes upon her, but she studiously concentrated on the food.

The main course was a homely meal of lamb chops, with roast potatoes and fresh vegetables, but she ate sparingly, her mind on the news she dreaded—news of Craig's engagement.

She was given the opportunity to mention Alec when Dr Tunstall boomed at her: 'I suppose you miss the social life of the big cities? Must be dull for you here.'

His gaze was watchful, as was Craig's, and Rosemary thought how much the two big men resembled each other.

'No, I don't miss it that much. Not really,' she faltered. 'Sometimes at weekends, I can go back. Or—or Alec might come down here. He phones quite often.' She gave Craig a brilliant smile, but didn't get the reaction she expected. His eyes were hooded, giving nothing away.

The reaction came from Dr Tunstall. 'Alec?' he roared. 'I thought you'd given him the push! He wouldn't fit in here, my dear. We humble village folk would soon give *him* the run-around!' He chuckled at his own wit, but Rosemary and Craig did not join in.

Rosemary made a vague gesture, trying to indicate that she knew Alec didn't belong there. 'He has his own business, Doctor. It isn't easy for him to get away.'

As she spoke, she wondered why Alec hadn't bothered any more. He, like Craig Dean, wasn't the sort to give up easily. It was vaguely annoying that he didn't care enough. A shadow crossed her face, but the doctors were, by now, talking shop again, and Rosemary turned her attention to Mrs Tunstall.

They were relaxing over coffee when Lyn arrived, complete with a freshly washed and brushed Steve. Rosemary's gaze went accusingly to Craig, but he was already welcoming the new-comers.

Lyn was pressed to sit down with them, but she refused, giving an oddly shy smile. 'No, we won't have anything, thank you. I knew you'd be at supper, and that's why I waited. We—we didn't want to be any trouble. Did we, Steve?'

The boy dutifully shook his head, and Rose-mary's heart went out to him. Impulsively she held out her hand.

'Come on, Steve. While Mummy's talking, you can come to see Spike.'

She took the boy through to the kitchen, where Steve and Spike greeted each other enthusiastically. The boy prattled on while Rosemary automatically got on with washing the dishes. It had been a lovely meal, and it wasn't the Tunstalls' fault that she hadn't much appetite.

She had barely started when Mrs Tunstall came out to give her a hand, followed, to Rosemary's surprise, by Dr Tunstall.

'Left them alone,' the doctor rumbled, and Rosemary nodded. Naturally they would want to be alone; they had many plans to make.

Between them they did the dishes and tidied the kitchen. To Rosemary's amusement, Dr Tunstall donned a flowered apron to tackle the drying-up. Steve seemed content to stay with them, so they all sat in the roomy kitchen chatting generally, until Craig appeared.

If Rosemary wondered why she had seen nothing of Steve during half-term, she found out the reason. He had been staying with his father.

'And Auntie, too, at Hastings,' he told them. 'But it was too cold to go in the water. Daddy said he'd take me swimming in the summer, but Auntie said he wouldn't be there,' he finished sadly.

Tears pricked Rosemary's eyes. Daddy wouldn't be there, yet Steve would have a new daddy by then. Of course Craig would take him swimming. 'You never know,' she said lightly, ruffling his dark hair. 'Someone might take you to the beach next summer.'

'We went this year, Daddy Craig took us,' Steve announced, and Mrs Tunstall gave him a cuddle.

'*He* won't always be around, either, Steve,' she said firmly. 'He's a busy man. Doctors always are.'

Steve nodded. 'I'm going to be a doctor, just like Daddy Craig. When I grow up, that is. It won't be for a while yet,' he added seriously.

It was then that they noticed Craig in the doorway. His gaze was intent, and Rosemary bent to stroke Spike. She felt they had outstayed their welcome; the Tunstalls would want to sit with Lyn and the boy.

She left shortly afterwards, without seeing Lyn again, giving as her reason for leaving the fact that Alec might ring.

This time she got some reaction from Craig. She saw his lips tighten, then he turned abruptly and made a fuss of Spike, so Rosemary was unable to read his expression.

Aunt Lizzie *and* Craig turned up on Rosemary's doorstep the following morning. Rosemary had done her stint at the Saturday morning clinic, then hurried home to take Spike for a long walk before lunch.

Although the nights were drawing in, and were bitterly cold, the last few days had been bright and sunny. That brought frost at night, but it certainly brightened up the days. There was *some* warmth in the sunshine, and Rosemary determined that Spike must have as many long walks as possible before the winter really started.

The sunshine had put paid to her feeling that late autumn was a depressing time, and she saw now how the autumn tints beautified the trees. Some were partly bare, and the Forest was littered with a carpet of red, gold and bronze. It was all so much prettier than the cities and, at times, she felt that she never wanted to leave Hurstfield and Ashdown Forest.

Aunt Lizzie arrived first. Surprised but pleased, Rosemary hugged her.

Aunt Lizzie beamed. 'I had to talk to you,' she explained, her shrewd gaze assessing her.

Rosemary knew she looked pale and rather wan, but a brisk walk with the dog would soon cure that. Her aunt didnt want to join in the ramble, so she sat with her for a while, drinking tea and talking about old times.

'You always were a stubborn girl,' Aunt Lizzie remarked conversationally, and Rosemary chuckled.

'And I've grown into a stubborn woman! I'm afraid I can't change, even for you.'

'It's Alec—he's pining for you.' The remark came out of the blue, and Rosemary paused in the act of breaking up a digestive biscuit for Spike.

'He isn't the type of man to pine,' she said crisply. 'He's probably got a girl in his bed already —the sort you don't have to marry first,' she added, and Aunt Lizzie snorted.

'He may have. I don't enquire into his sex life, my dear. A man has his needs, of course, but it's *you* he loves.'

Dear Aunt Lizzie, always making excuses for the man! Rosemary smiled gently at her. 'I have *my* needs as well, and if he——'

Spike growled, his eyes on the front door, then his tail began to wag as someone rang the bell.

He must have recognised the sound of a friend's car, or seen someone he knew pass the window, but the only person Rosemary could think of was young Steve or Mandy Fairley.

It was Craig, and Spike sniffed around him eagerly. Craig's eyes met Aunt Lizzie's over the top of Rosemary's head. 'I'm sorry, I didn't know you had visitors, Sister,' he said formally.

Flustered, Rosemary invited him in. For one moment she thought it was a social call, but his use of the term 'Sister' put paid to that.

Craig and Aunt Lizzie sized each other up, both apparently liking what they saw. Aunt Lizzie patted the settee invitingly, and with a relaxed grin Craig joined her, the dog following at his heels.

Within half an hour Aunt Lizzie had Craig's whole life story out of him, including his so-far frustrated wish to work in the Third World Countries.

'Out there in the Sudan and Ethiopia they're crying out for help!' he insisted. Rosemary stirred his coffee before handing him the mug, and Craig sipped it absently, his thoughts many miles away.

'So you won't be staying in this delightful village, Doctor?' Aunt Lizzie was nothing if not persistent, and Rosemary felt embarrassed at the way she probed and pried into Craig's plans for the future.

He shrugged wearily, then ran his fingers through his already untidy hair. He still needed a haircut, and Rosemary hoped her sharp-eyed and sharp-tongued aunt wouldn't mention it.

It was too much to hope. 'You must let me cut your hair, doctor,' Aunt Lizzie offered, setting down her mug with a determined air. 'I don't suppose you get time to go to the barber's.'

To Rosemary's amazement, Craig submitted meekly to her aunt's ministrations. Aunt Lizzie spread out several sheets of newspaper on the floor, then ordered Rosemary to fetch the Hoover. 'Go on, there's a good girl. Oh, and I'll have your scissors.'

Sighing, Rosemary produced the scissors she had once been so eager to use on Craig's hair, then fetched her best towel to drape around his shoulders.

He thanked her gravely, then their eyes met and they both chuckled. 'I'm sorry about Aunt Lizzie,' Rosemary apologised, then the lady in question hove into view, the sleeves of her smart blouse rolled up, and a plastic apron protecting her skirt.

Rosemary watched in admiration as the work proceeded. Aunt Lizzie had a great deal of skill, and used to cut Rosemary's hair in days long gone. 'Would you cut mine when you've finished?' she asked, as the barbering drew to a close.

Aunt Lizzie looked scandalised, but it was Craig who told Rosemary firmly that her hair was beautiful as it was.

'Is it?' she asked, stunned. She was proud of her long, fine flaxen hair, but since she wore it up on duty, she didn't think he had ever noticed it. Now it was loose, and with her plump face free from make-up, she looked about twenty.

'You have lovely hair, Rosemary, and I couldn't possibly cut it. The ends just need trimming occasionally, that's all,' her aunt said decisively, and Rosemary didn't argue. She knew better.

She duly admired Craig's new hairstyle. 'It's the first time I've seen you looking so tidy,' she added, with a smile, and he chuckled.

'I do look rather a mess sometimes, don't I?' He glanced down ruefully at his faded jeans and ancient checked shirt.

To Rosemary's eyes he looked perfect. The evening before, he had worn a dark grey, neatly-pressed suit with a white shirt and pale grey tie. The tie looked suspiciously like silk, and Rosemary wondered who had bought it for him. He wasn't a man who took an interest in being fashionable, yet yesterday proved that he could make the effort.

Even in jeans and old shirt, he was irresistible, and Rosemary turned away, that awful ache in her heart came back.

'Don't go, Rosemary. I've got a few hours free. It's time Spike had another good walk.' Craig bent to pat the mongrel. 'She neglects you, Spike. You need at least ten miles a day!'

Aunt Lizzie chortled. 'I can't see our city-dwelling Rosemary walking ten miles, but you can try! Oh, will you be back for lunch?'

'I thought about taking Rosemary out to lunch, then giving Spike a good run afterwards.' Craig consulted his watch. 'It's nearly twelve now, Aunt Lizzie. Will you join us?'

But Aunt Lizzie refused his offer, and assured them she would find enough to eat in the house.

So, with Spike in the back seat, they set out. It was a beautiful day, and if it hadn't been for her heartache, Rosemary would have enjoyed the drive more. Probably she needed feeding. A glass of shandy and a good pub meal, and she would be fine.

They lunched at a tiny pub just outside Crowborough, which was on the edge of Ashdown Forest. Afterwards, they drove to an area of unenclosed woodland. More than half Ashdown Forest belonged to private owners, the remainder being common land where people could walk freely. Some of the most beautiful woodland was open, and Spike, perhaps scenting wild creatures, was eager to be off, straining at the leash.

'He wants his walk, poor chap,' remarked Craig, turning to Rosemary. His smile was tender, intimate, and she pretended to be engrossed in the scenery, wanting to avoid his gaze.

'Rosemary?' That one word was little more than a whisper, a breath of summer breeze, the substance of a dream.

'Craig, please——' she began, determined not to let him see how much she cared. Yet when he put his arm around her shoulders and drew her head down, she capitulated. All her good resolutions vanished as if they had never been.

With a little sigh, she rested her head against his chest and closed her eyes. Craig kissed her eyelids, his lips moving tantalisingly down her face to her throat.

'Craig, don't,' she murmured.

'Doctor never does,' he laughed softly, and her eyes shot open.

'That's right. You're supposed to make advances to brunettes. They——' She stopped, a shadow crossing her face. Lyn, the dark star, must be cruising overhead. She shivered, feeling the other woman's presence even here, on the border of the Garden of Eden.

'Rosemary, what is it? Tell me!' Craig insisted, but she shook her head, the fine, flyaway hair obstructing his vision as she did so.

'Come on, then, let's give Spike a run before it gets too cold.' His tone was brusque, and a chastened Rosemary followed him.

'We mustn't be too long,' she said to his obdurate back. 'Aunt Lizzie said to be back before dark. I expect she feels nervous in a strange house.'

'Yes, that's a pity. I was hoping to show you the A. A. Milne territory today, but we'll leave it for now.' Craig's voice was less unfriendly now, and she took heart from it.

The eastern edge of the Forest was high land, Crowborough Beacon reaching over seven hundred feet, but Craig headed unerringly for slightly lower ground, plunging into a small wood, while Spike forged eagerly ahead, Rosemary holding firmly to his extending lead.

Here it was wild. Holly bushes, brambles and

gorse grew in profusion, but the bridleway was well kept.

It was lonely, too. The only people they met on their walk was a horse-rider. Much of the Forest area was favoured by horse-riders, and Rosemary gazed after him wistfully.

'There are stables around here if you ride.' Craig stopped and waited for her.

She shook her head firmly. 'No, I don't ride—I just like to watch them. They seem so free, as if the whole world belonged to them,' she added, feeling foolish.

Craig pressed her hand understandingly. 'I know what you mean. Unfortunately, it isn't as idyllic a life as it seems. Illegal riding is a problem in the Forest.' He hesitated, blue eyes resting on her pale face.

Rosemary tensed, wondering what was coming.

'Do you intend taking up with Scott again?'

'Scott? Oh, Alec! I—I've never really left him,' she said, with a shaky attempt at a laugh. 'He still phones. And writes sometimes. We——' she searched for words that would sound convincing, 'we decided on a trial separation, Craig. After all, Alec and I move in different circles. We're whole worlds apart, really, and——'

'What conclusions have you come to?' His tone was polite, only vaguely interested, and, perversely, Rosemary felt let down.

'We've decided that absence *does* make the heart grow fonder. He'll be coming down soon,' she added rashly. 'Then—then we have plans to make.'

Rosemary shot him an anxious glance from under half-closed lashes. Let Craig believe that all was well with her love life. He need not think that she was brokenhearted because he was marrying Lyn. Nor should he think that he could flirt with her, as a more interesting sideline. If he married the dull Lyn, then he must put up with her. No way was he making use of Sister Miller!

To her chagrin, he made no further comment, beyond telling her they must get a move on if they were to be back before dark.

Craig had promised her a sweeping view of the Forest, and he kept that promise on the drive home. A reluctant Spike had been persuaded back to the car, and after a drive of some miles they came to the spot Craig wanted to show her.

The air was turning chill now, but they both wore thick anoraks, and it was still daylight. They had plenty of time to get back to the cottage. Rosemary hoped Aunt Lizzie would have a hot meal awaiting them, and that Craig could be persuaded to stay.

Of course it was masochism on her part. Knowing she could not have him, she yet spent as much time in his company as possible. She was sad away from him, even sadder than when they were together.

They were on the western fringes of the Forest now, Craig explained, though Rosemary had no idea exactly where they were. Although born in the country, she had never had occasion to visit Ashdown Forest before. The main Eastbourne to London road ran through the Forest, true, but it was a road with dangerous bends, and it needed concentrated driving. She'd never had time to really notice the Forest itself as she sped along.

Now, a whole new world was opening up before her.

Craig led her past an ancient church and into an even older churchyard. 'Hardly a romantic vantage point,' he commented dryly, 'but the view is superb. When the wind isn't howling,' he added, seeing Rosemary shiver.

She tensed when his arm settled about her shoulder, but when she tried to shrug away his arm, he merely tightened his grip. She wondered if he knew the pain he caused her, but of course he didn't. How could he know?

Her gaze followed Craig's pointed finger. Far away, many miles below, was the basin of the river Ouse, with a tributary of the river flowing down a wooded ghyll or ravine.

Pale winter sunlight danced on the river, turning the scene to a painting of silvery blue, emerald green, and gold, and Rosemary caught her breath at such loveliness. She didn't need to visit the tropical isle she sometimes longed for. Everything she needed was here in England—including the man she loved.

They descended again, Craig taking her hand. 'It's so beautiful,' Rosemary sighed, saddened yet uplifted by so much natural beauty. Within her was a great yearning, a fervent wish to be part of the landscape, to remain there for ever—with Craig.

Tears sprang to her eyes, but she bent down and made a fuss of Spike so that Craig shouldn't see the tears and wonder at them. He was too perceptive by far.

He was waiting for her at the car. Even the car parks were landscaped here, and Rosemary paused for one last look around. Ever after she would associate this place with Craig, and intended to return as a sort of pilgrimage.

Busy with her thoughts, she was unable to escape Craig's embrace. He must have been brooding about Alec, and about her remarks concerning her future. Then the breath left her body as Craig pulled her into his arms, his mouth descending forcefully upon hers.

When he let her go, her breathing was ragged. Yet he showed no mercy, his fingers digging into her upper arms as he glared down at her.

'I wish you joy of Alec Scott!' he ground out. 'I think you're admirably suited—two arrogant, unfeeling city-dwellers, who care for no one but themselves!'

Rosemary gasped, then struggled to find words hurtful enough to hurl at him.

She wasn't allowed the chance. Craig's breathing was as uneven as her own, but his words were decisive enough: 'If you're going to return to the Midlands, do it now, Sister Miller! Bring in your letter of resignation on Monday—it'll give us time to get a district nurse before the winter epidemics *really* start.'

'Now just you listen to me, Craig Dean!' she began hotly. 'I have——'

'That will do, Sister!' His tone brooked no further argument. 'I need a district nurse I can rely on, not one who can't decide what she wants from life—or even which man she wants,' he added nastily.

With grave politeness he held open the car door for her.

CHAPTER TEN

THEY arrived back as darkness fell. Aunt Lizzie fussed over Spike, carrying him off to the kitchen to be measured. 'He'll need a coat for the really bad weather,' she announced brightly. 'I can start on one when I get home. I like to keep a bit of knitting on the go,' she called over her shoulder, apparently keen to leave Rosemary and Craig alone.

However, Craig refused Aunt Lizzie's offer of supper, and he was grim-faced as Rosemary saw him out. He hesitated on the doorstep, his face half illuminated by the porch light.

'Rosemary—if things don't turn out as planned, remember that I'm always here.'

She nodded. She wanted to cling to him, tell him she needed him, that she couldn't live without him. Yet always between them came the image of Lyn —a sad, rather forlorn figure who really *did* need tender loving care. She was vicious, manipulating, yes, but Rosemary couldn't help feeling sorry for her, just as she had felt sorry for Spike. That was what came of being too soft-hearted!

'Thank you, Craig,' she whispered. She was prepared for the good night kiss he planted on her brow, but not prepared for the wave of longing that swept over her. 'Craig——' she said brokenly. But he was gone.

Cursing her weak, womanly body, she closed the door with a bang.

158

She was silent during the meal, and to her surprise, her aunt did not comment.

It was when they were washing the dishes afterwards that Aunt Lizzie dropped her bombshell. 'I was supposed to phone Alec and tell him you're still pining for him,' she announced. 'But I can see you're not,' she added dryly, before Rosemary could comment.

'Yes, you can tell him that I'm definitely *not* pining,' Rosemary emphasised with a sad smile. 'At least, not for Alec.'

Aunt Lizzie snorted. 'You're a fool, Rosemary. It's that big fair man, isn't it? *He's* wrapped up in his work. Going off to Africa the first chance he gets, I reckon. Africa, indeed!'

That 'big fair man' did not love her, and the sooner she could put him out of her mind, the better—something Rosemary found extraordinarily difficult to do.

The whooping cough intensified towards the end of the following week, and Rosemary had no time to dwell on her heartache, or even to notice Craig as other than a GP.

Although it was rather early in the winter for a full-scale epidemic, the weather had suddenly worsened. One day it was late autumn, with pale, weak sunshine; the next it was sleeting and bitterly cold. It remained that way until the beginning of December.

The epidemic spread quickly, though Rosemary couldn't help thinking how much worse it would have been in a congested city. In Hurstfield and the neighbouring villages it was bad enough.

For a time, the village schools were closed, though it was mainly babies who were infected. With several small children in some families, it was hardly surprising that the disease went through them all.

Whooping cough had its highest mortality rate in those under one year old, but there had been only the one death in Hurstfield. If that poor child had been immunised, he could well have been alive still. It made it worse for the parents that he had been an only child. Fortunately the mother was young, so Rosemary knew it wouldn't be long before she started a new family, and put the agony of bereavement behind her.

For Mrs Mitchell, it wasn't so easy. She was one of Craig's patients, a first-time mother at just gone forty. Older mothers generally tended to be more sensible, and Rosemary wondered why Tim Mitchell hadn't been immunised. He had been protected against nothing at all, according to his medical records.

Tim had just had a paroxysmal attack when Rosemary called, though Mrs Mitchell assured her the attacks were getting less. He was sitting in his cot, in a stuffy, overheated bedroom. He was a usually lively ten-month-old, and Rosemary had met him before when she had called with some elastic stockings for Mrs Mitchell's elderly mother. Now his eyes were streaming, and he looked so unhappy that Rosemary longed to cuddle him to her, tell him that the worst was over.

'I've been giving him small meals after each bout of sickness, Sister, just like the young doctor told me,' Mrs Mitchell announced, and Rosemary nodded approvingly.

She didn't want to quarrel with the woman, who was clearly doing her best, and she praised Mrs Mitchell's care of him. 'He's looking better, I think,' she said cautiously, 'but once the fever is past, these kiddies need fresh air. I wonder if it isn't rather too warm in here for him?'

Mrs Mitchell looked doubtful. 'Mother said to keep him warm, Sister. She's over eighty, and she's seen all these diseases before, you know. Brought up a family of seven, she did,' she added smugly, as if that settled the matter.

'I suppose none of you had whatever immunisations were available then?' Rosemary wasn't surprised when the answer was a firm shake of the head.

'We managed without, all of us. Only lost one, my mother did, and that was with diphtheria.'

Rosemary was glad to hear that, because it gave her a chance to drive home a point. 'Years ago, when your mother was bringing up her own family, deaths from diphtheria were frequent, and cases of the disease ran into thousands,' she pointed out. 'Yet, thirty years later, cases notified were less than a hundred, because more and more mothers decided on immunisation for their infants. Your mother was fortunate in losing only *one* child, Mrs Mitchell. So you see, immunisation *does* help,' she finished. 'I'll let you get on now—you'll want to feed Tim before he starts coughing again.'

Small feeds had to be given at frequent intervals, and the child actively coaxed or bribed to eat. If the meal was given as soon after a bout of 'whooping' as possible, the food had time to be assimilated before the onset of another bout. With very small babies, dehydration was a problem, as it was among deprived families. Rosemary had no fears for Tim, though. He was, if anything, overweight, and had always been well cared for. Mrs Mitchell's husband was well into his fifties, and for them Tim must remain an only child.

She had seen virtually nothing of Craig for the past fortnight, and she knew from Gwen Sayers that he was called out all hours of the day and night. Although Dr Tunstall was reasonably fit, Craig naturally wished to save the older man from night calls as much as possible.

Rosemary worried about him constantly. Only the belief that Lyn was looking after him kept her away. The Tunstalls too probably fed him at intervals. They wouldn't see him become rundown, though whether he got enough sleep was doubtful.

A disappointed Aunt Lizzie had gone back home to her budgie, convinced that Rosemary had gone mad. To throw herself away on a mere doctor when she could have the rich and sophisticated Alec Scott was inconceivable to her. Aunt Lizzie's parting words to Rosemary had been: 'He'll never marry you, Rosemary. You know that, don't you?'

Rosemary had agreed that she knew, and didn't expect marriage, anyway.

One afternoon, after a particularly gruelling day, she kicked off her shoes, and relaxed in her velvet dressing-gown. The first thing she always did on reaching home was to remove her clothes, wrap herself in the dressing-gown, then put the kettle on.

Spike, of course, had to be let into the garden, but apart from that, she could relax for ten minutes or so before showering and changing.

The doorbell rang just as she was nodding off, and she jerked upright, not realising at first where the sound was coming from. Then it rang again, several times, and Spike growled.

With a sigh, Rosemary went to the front door and called out: 'Who is it?' She didn't like opening the door after dark, even here in the country. In any case, the dressing-gown wasn't exactly regulation uniform!

Craig Dean's deep, masculine voice answered her, and reluctantly she inched the door open. Spike whined eagerly, his long tail thudding against the door.

Craig raised a brow when he saw her, a little smile tugging at the corners of his wide mouth. 'Really, Sister Miller! Is this the way to receive guests?'

Face flushed, she locked the door after him, giving it a final thump to relieve her feelings. 'You aren't a guest. Not an invited one, anyway. I'm off duty,' she added firmly. She was rather afraid she would weaken and offer him coffee, and her brusqueness hid the depth of feeling she had for him.

'Thank you, I *will* sit down,' Craig said amiably, crossing to the settee, where she herself had been sitting only seconds before. 'Ah, this is good! Your settee is a lot more comfortable than mine,' he sighed, stretching his long legs out in front of the fire.

Spike lay across his feet, and Rosemary silently

cursed the animal's slavish obedience. Even Spike was in league against her!

'I'll make you some coffee, Doctor.' Her tone was unwelcoming, for she could not afford to let him know how much she wanted him to stay. 'Then I must shower and change. Spike hasn't had his walk yet.'

Spike sat up, his tail starting again, and a satisfied Rosemary withdrew to the kitchen. The dog wouldn't rest now that he had heard the magic word 'walk', so Craig wouldn't be able to rest, either. The very last thing she wanted was for him to fall asleep in front of her fire.

While the coffee was on, she was tempted to go upstairs and don whatever clothing she could find. She was naked except for the dressing-gown, and felt vulnerable. Yet that would be an admission to Craig that she was uncomfortable and embarrassed in his presence, and she wasn't going to admit that. If she made the coffee just warm enough to drink, she would soon be rid of him.

Craig *was* asleep when she returned with the tray of coffee and biscuits. Her gaze softened as she watched him. In sleep he looked younger, vulnerable even. The thought crossed her mind that he must have been an adorable child, then she found those pale blue eyes fixed upon her.

'You're awake, then. Good,' she said crisply, setting down the tray on the coffee-table, trying not to bend over too much as she did so. She didn't want to give him an unauthorised view of long, sturdy legs!

Craig chuckled, evidently aware of her predicament. 'If I had the energy, Sister Miller, I'd make passionate love to you,' he murmured silkily.

Rosemary placed the cup and saucer in his hand and glared. 'It's just as well you're too tired!' she snapped, seating herself in the armchair. The springs protested, and she glared even more.

'That chair needs replacing, Sister,' said Craig with a sly grin, and she couldn't help smiling.

'I rather think Sister Miller has got heavier!' she said ruefully. 'All that nourishing winter food. The springs were all right when I moved here.' She cast a critical eye over his own frame. 'I've gained the weight you've lost, I think.'

Craig shrugged, surveying her from under his long, thick lashes. Despite her good intentions, she felt love for him overwhelming her, and she stared into the artificial flames of the fire, clasping her arms around her knees like a child.

'I've a favour to ask of you,' he said, setting down his empty cup, and she sighed inwardly.

Naturally he wanted a favour. There was no other reason to call on her, but for a short while she had believed he wanted some tender loving care, that he saw her cottage as an oasis in a desert of overwork. 'Yes?' she kept her voice neutral, wondering why Lyn couldn't help out if he needed a nurse.

A series of meetings had been arranged by the surgery. They were mainly Craig's idea, and Rosemary knew about them, of course. The health visitor, Margaret Gearing, would be there, but Rosemary had assumed that she herself wouldn't be needed.

Craig wanted to talk to parents of young children, principally parents with babies, about the advantages of immunisation. 'I need help, Rosemary. From you,' he said simply.

How could she refuse? Her lips curved into a faint smile. 'What about Margaret?' she asked aloud. 'She's had a lot more experience than I——'

'You're better with people than she is, Rosemary.' His eyes smiled into hers. 'I wish you were fully dressed,' he added with a wry smile, 'then I could kiss you. As it is . . .'

He left the sentence unfinished, and she coloured swiftly. 'You'd better go, Dr Dean. I have to change and take Spike for his walk.'

'Yes, Sister.' Craig rose, his gaze thoughtful as it rested on her flushed face. 'Once the winter surge of whooping cough, 'flu, etc, is over, I'll be able to finalise my plans for the future.'

A rain-cloud settled on Rosemary, but she tried to smile it away. Plans for his future—his and Lyn's.

Rosemary attended several meetings. One was in the evening and intended for fathers, mainly, but the others were at the surgery, where mothers could bring their offspring. They were well attended, and fruitful, Rosemary considered. The epidemic of whooping cough had caused parents to re-think.

She wished Craig wouldn't try to do so much, though. He was wearing himself out, as GPs so often did. Dr Tunstall too was tired, and he had confided to Rosemary that he was looking forward to his retirement.

It was when she saw the indigestion tablets that Rosemary really became alarmed. She was at the

Tunstalls' for supper again. As usual, the doctors were out on their rounds, though things were better now. The whooping cough was slackening off and, luxury of luxuries, Dr Tunstall had just taken on another partner, a female doctor. Old ladies often preferred a lady doctor, and this one was young and keen. Her husband was a local man, and Rosemary couldn't help being glad that the pretty young doctor was happily married!

Influenza still raged, and there was the usual crop of colds, broncho-pneumonia, bronchitis, shingles, that sort of thing. Certainly enough to keep the group busy.

Rosemary was in the kitchen feeding Spike when she saw the tablets. They were marked with Craig's name and were a proprietary brand, innocuous enough. She frowned, before picking them up.

Mrs Tunstall saw her. 'They're Craig's. He isn't eating regular meals, you know.'

When eventually Craig arrived, he looked ill and drawn. He ate very little, his aunt coaxing him the way Aunt Lizzie used to coax Rosemary to eat when she was young. It would have been amusing if it wasn't so sad.

Because it wasn't far, Rosemary and Spike had walked to the house; it gave them both some much-needed exercise. Craig insisted on seeing them home. 'I can collect my car tomorrow. I need fresh air and exercise, too,' he smiled. His already thin face was thinner, but those blue, blue eyes were as bright as ever, and Rosemary's heart swelled with love for him.

They walked arm-in-arm through the cold, still night. Even in winter there was a kind of magic in the air, though it may have been because she was with the man she loved. He *needed* her! Why couldn't he see that? *But*, a small, charitable voice whispered, Lyn needs *him*. You're tough, Rosemary. Lyn's need is greater than yours.

'Good old Sister Miller.' Rosemary wasn't aware that she had spoken aloud until Craig chuckled.

'That's absolutely right. Good old Sister Miller!'

She laughed, too, but wasn't amused. That was all she would ever be to Craig Dean.

'Granny Cole's poorly again,' Craig remarked as he settled himself in front of her fire, a little later. He seemed so at home there that Rosemary, unthinkingly, put out a hand and stroked his brow.

His eyes met hers unsmilingly. 'I won't be responsible for the consequences if you do that again, Rosemary,' he said quietly, and she jerked her hand away as if she had touched red-hot metal.

'I—I'm sorry,' she said stiffly, trying not to show how his words hurt. 'I'll make some coffee. Excuse me.' She fled into the kitchen, closing the door behind her.

The tears she always kept so carefully hidden could be dammed up no longer, and with a gulping sob she hid herself in the big, roomy larder and just howled. She cried until she could cry no more. The flood became a trickle, then stopped altogether. Her chest hurt with the effect, and her eyes felt sore and gritty, and were probably puffy, as well.

'Rosemary.' Craig must have arrived in the middle of the flood, because she hadn't heard the kitchen door open. He cradled her gently to his chest, and she snuggled into him. 'Rosemary, my love.'

Rosemary, my love. Oh, if only she was! Abruptly she pulled herself free. 'I'll get that coffee now —unless you want something stronger?' Her voice held only the faintest quiver, and she was rather proud of the way she could meet his intent gaze.

'It all depends what the "something stronger" is,' he said softly.

'Well, there's some whisky—Aunt Lizzie left it in case I get a cold! Then there's what she calls the "medicinal" brandy! Oh, and a bottle of port.'

'*Port?*' he echoed.

'That's Aunt Lizzie as well, I'm afraid,' Rosemary admitted, with a smile.

'For a lady who was staying only one night, she certainly came well stocked!' he laughed.

'She likes her little tipple,' Rosemary admitted, as she put the kettle on. 'I'm sorry the coffee's only instant—my percolator broke down.'

'I'd rather have cocoa or something in that line, if it's no trouble, Rosemary.'

She swung round, suddenly remembering the indigestion tablets. She mustn't let him know she had seen them. 'Would hot milk suit? That's what I was going to have myself. Or there's some Horlicks?'

Craig settled for the hot milk, and afterwards they sat companionably beside the fire, Spike lying stretched out on his side on the pretty handmade rug.

Craig dozed, and Rosemary tried not to move. The poor dear needed his sleep—he might be called out again tonight. He—— No, she recalled hearing Mrs Tunstall say that it was the new doctor's night on call.

Ought she to waken him? If he was to be allowed an undisturbed night at home, it wouldn't do him any good to sleep now. He wouldn't be fit for the morning.

Rosemary sat beside him, watching the rise and fall of his chest. His old tartan shirt was open at the neck, and there was a button missing from it. The comfortable old cords were creased and well worn, and his hair was growing. He would soon need the ministrations of Aunt Lizzie again!

Overcome by tenderness, she snuggled up against him, resting her weary head on the broad expanse of shoulder, and closed her eyes.

The three of them slept on till past midnight, and it was Spike whining to go out that woke Rosemary. She sat up, her neck stiff and her arm in a cramp where she had been lying on it. Craig surveyed her from his more comfortable position. Wry humour lit his gaze. 'We're getting like a couple of old biddies, Rosemary! Dropping off to sleep whenever we sit in front of a fire.'

'I'll just let Spike out. Then he'll probably want a meal.' Rosemary's voice was distant, cool. She didn't want Craig to guess how much she had enjoyed the session in his arms.

He glanced at his watch. 'Good God, it's after twelve! That greedy hound won't want feeding now, Rosemary.'

'I wouldn't be too sure about that!' Spike was willing to eat at any time.

It was beginning to snow, the first real snow of the winter, though they'd had plenty of sleet. Rosemary stood and watched the pretty flakes coming down, while Spike did his rounds of the small garden. It wasn't much and would probably be gone by morning. Even as she watched by the light of the torch, the flakes melted on reaching earth.

She closed and bolted the door after Spike, then bent to dry him. 'It's snowing, Craig,' she called softly, wondering if he had gone back to sleep.

He had. Leaving Spike to enjoy an unexpected supper-cum-breakfast, Rosemary peered around the door. Craig was stretched out on the settee again, full-length this time. There wasn't room for his long legs, and his feet dangled over the edge —wearing a pair of nondescript socks that she longed to darn.

She crept upstairs to get a blanket and a pillow for him, then made him as comfortable as she could. She took a blanket for herself, and decided to sit up in the armchair for what remained of the night.

The only light came from the fire, which she turned low. She felt Spike come through from the kitchen and stretch out at her feet.

Then she must have dozed. The next thing she knew, she was in Craig's arms on the settee. With a contented smile she curled up against him, and he chuckled softly.

'I couldn't let you sit in that chair all night,' he murmured, as he nuzzled her cheek.

'Don't,' she whispered, as his lips nibbled experimentally at her earlobe. 'I might get to like it!'

Despite the fact that they were both fully clothed, she felt desire stir within her. Her heart was performing a crazy little jig, and she felt dizzy with longing for him. She had to fight it. But how?

Craig made it harder for her. He pressed her palm to his lips, then began to kiss her fingers, one by one.

'Craig, don't, *please*!' Rosemary attempted to snatch her hand again, but he wouldn't let go. 'Rosemary,' he murmured huskily, 'I can't do without you.'

For one exciting, breathtaking moment, Rosemary believed him. She thought he meant that he loved her, but the words of love never came, and the excitement and the desire subsided.

Of course he meant nothing of the kind. If he meant he couldn't do without her as a woman, it was because he needed the physical release that lovemaking would bring him. It was more than likely, though, that he meant he needed her in her professional capacity. He was right there. At present he couldn't do without the reliable Sister Miller.

Bitterly, she pushed against his chest. 'I had no right to . . . to lead you on, Craig. I'm sorry.' Saying sorry was hardly adequate, but she had to put a stop to it, otherwise they would have ended up in her bed. Such an ending was inevitable. She wanted to belong to Craig, yearned to give him the love and tenderness that he so badly needed, but always there was a shadow of Lyn.

Hadn't she seen them together only two days before? Rosemary's blood boiled at the memory. Lyn had been laughing up at Craig, while young Steve gambolled at their side. It was so like a real family scene that Rosemary's heart had ached.

Craig ought to apologise to *her*, not the other

way round! He had no business stringing two
women along like this.

'I've decided to marry Alec,' she said swiftly,
before he could take her into his arms again.

'Lucky old Alec.' Craig's tone was light, mock-
ingly so, yet underneath she could hear the anger,
the hurt. Let him hurt. It was time he had a taste of
his own medicine!

All her tender feelings for him vanished. Hadn't
he been holding her in reserve all these weeks,
taking her out whenever Lyn wasn't available?

'I even took that dog in because Lyn didn't want
him!' she cried, feeling exceedingly hard done by.

'Lyn? Were we talking about Lyn? I thought the
subject under discussion was that Scott fellow—
England's answer to Robert Redford,' Craig added
bitterly.

'That's a spiteful remark!' she flared. 'Just because he's tall, dark and handsome and—and rich
and——'

'Well dressed,' Craig added.

'Yes, he *is*!' Rosemary gave Craig's old clothes a
contemptuous look.

He chuckled. 'GPs wear their oldest clothes
for visiting patients, Rosemary. You know that,
surely?'

She nodded, feeling dreadful. 'I'm sorry, Craig, I
didn't mean to compare you unfavourably with
Alec.'

'It's only hospital consultants who wear Savile
Row suits to go on duty!' he told her, against her
ear.

'I know, Craig, and I'm sorry. I didn't mean to be
unkind, and you not well!'

'Of course I'm well, Rosemary. Fit as a fiddle, me!' he joked, but she wasn't deceived.

She ran her fingers down his thin cheek. 'You're losing weight, and what about those indigestion tablets? Oh, Craig, if anything should happen to you, I——' Her voice trailed off, and it was just as well. She had so very nearly told him she loved him!

'You weren't supposed to know about the tablets. My aunt cooked me an over-rich meal one evening, that was all.' Craig's tone brooked no argument, but Rosemary couldn't believe that one meal had caused him to suffer indigestion ever since. It was more likely that he had a gastric ulcer coming.

'You'd better go back to Lyn, hadn't you?' She sniffed, searching for her hankie. Twice in one day the big, practical Sister Miller had broken down in front of him. He must be getting weary of it. It wasn't as if she could cry *prettily*, like some girls.

'And you must go back to Alec,' he said quietly.

Quick to seize on that excuse, she got up. 'Yes, yes, I must. He——'

'But before we go our separate ways, here's a little gift to remember me by.' Before Rosemary was aware of his intentions, Craig's mouth closed over hers, and her body was crushed against his powerful frame. Waves of longing washed over her, the desire turning her blood to liquid fire, and she clung to him for a moment, too weak to stand unaided.

'Craig,' she whispered brokenly, her own desire mounting as his kisses became more demanding.

'Rosemary, my love,' he murmured against her ear. 'I need you.'

Even though she knew he didn't love her, she so wanted to believe him. And he *did* need her. Why shouldn't they take a little pleasure while they could? Lyn would never know . . .

But I would, she thought. I would know, and I could never look Lyn in the face again.

Craig's lips trailed a line of kisses across her throat, and she felt her resolve weakening. 'No, Craig,' she whispered. 'there's Lyn . . .'

His eyes were still glazed with passion when they broke apart. He pushed his hands through his already mussed hair. 'Yes, there's Lyn. That's a problem I've nearly sorted out, thank God!' He hesitated, taking Rosemary's hand in his. 'I had hoped that——' Bleak eyes looked down into hers. 'I wish you and Alec all the best, Rosemary. Let me know what you'd like as a wedding present.'

Swiftly he pressed his lips against hers, then gathered up his shoes and jacket, and left. The front door closed quietly behind him, and Spike gazed up enquiringly at Rosemary.

'He's gone, Spike.' Rosemary bent to stroke the dog, her gaze taking in the rumpled blankets on the settee, the faint tang of aftershave, the lingering aroma of a warm, male body. 'The master's gone home,' she told the dog. 'He won't be back.'

After her unforgivable behaviour, he wouldn't come back. She had unwittingly led him on, then, when they might have enjoyed an hour stolen from Lyn, she'd told him she was going to marry Alec. What had possessed her to say such a thing?

Not that it mattered—he had Lyn.

CHAPTER ELEVEN

A WEEK or so later the whooping cough epidemic
died down, although there were still several very ill
children. One infant was in hospital with broncho-
pneumonia, one of the complications of the whooping cough, but he was expected to recover. The
occasional case was still being notified, but on
nothing like the previous scale, though sometimes
an epidemic could last for several months.

Rosemary was kept busy, both with advising on
the care of the stricken infants, and with her other
nursing duties. She made time, though, to visit Mrs
Ritter, Dave's mother. She was coping better with
the colostomy now, and Rosemary had introduced
her to an elderly woman in the next village, who
had also had a colostomy. It helped to know that
other people had similar operations.

The news about Dave was better too. Margaret
Gearing had followed him up, at Rosemary's request, and had contacted the university social
worker. It appeared that Dave had become involved with hard drugs, but wasn't physically
addicted to them. Because the other boys in his
year were experimenting with them, he had joined
in, but had managed to fight the habit before he
became hopelessly dependent upon them.

'Dave changed, Sister,' Mrs Ritter said tearfully.
'He was always a quiet boy, but he became secret-
ive, and quarrelsome sometimes. He lived in a

world of his own, but he's back in *this* world now, I think.'

'Any time he wants someone to talk to, I'll make myself available,' Rosemary assured her. 'Or Miss Gearing will be glad to help.'

She wondered, as she left, what had happened to the budding romance between Dave and young Mandy Fairley, but she got her answer the following Saturday.

Mandy called to take Spike out, and Rosemary was glad of her help. Being on call meant not going out unless she left word where she could be found, and it was difficult to take the dog out in such circumstances.

She had hot buttered scones and coffee awaiting Mandy when she returned, and to Rosemary's amazement, the girl tucked in eagerly.

When she tentatively mentioned Dave Ritter, she was met with a blank look. 'Oh, *Dave*!' Mandy said airily. 'I haven't seen him for about a month. They've broken up for Christmas now, I suppose.'

'Yes, I imagine they have,' Rosemary agreed quietly. 'Have you got a new interest now?'

Mandy giggled and blushed, before helping herself to another scone.

Rosemary smiled to herself. If Many *did* have a new love, he'd evidently told her she was too thin! Another almost-satisfied patient, she decided. Poor Dave, whatever his other problems, would have to find himself a new girl. At least Mandy didn't have anorexia nervosa, as Rosemary had feared. Her present hearty eating wasn't the sort one could describe as bulimia, either, so that was one problem less.

It wasn't until the middle of the following week that Rosemary realised she had lost another of her problems—Lyn Abbott.

Lyn wasn't at her desk when Rosemary called on Dr Tunstall just before evening surgery. That in itself was nothing unusual. Lyn often took unauthorised days off, leaving others to fit in her work as best they could.

Casting her mind back, Rosemary recalled that she hadn't seen Lyn since the previous Sunday. Her face clouded at the memory. When she saw them, they were all together on the steps of St Michael's, the parish church—Craig, Lyn and Steve, with the elderly vicar and one or two people she supposed were churchwardens. Evidently they had been making arrangements for some special event.

It could hardly be a wedding, since Lyn wasn't yet divorced. Or was she?

Rosemary's heart sank within her like a stone. That was that, then. Perhaps the divorce had been finalised, and Craig had asked the vicar if they could be married in church. Rosemary wasn't sure if it was allowed, but supposed they could have a church blessing; Craig was, after all, a figure of some standing in the community.

When she had seen Dr Tunstall, Rosemary half-heartedly searched for Craig. The waiting room was already filling up, but few of them appeared to be Craig's patients.

Gwen Sayers was doing a late duty, and Rosemary didn't want to ask her about Craig, so she merely had a brief word about the following morning's list, then left. She knew Gwen was dying to impart some important piece of information, but she didn't want to know. She would hear the 'good' news soon enough.

Her heart ached. So did her head. She'd read somewhere that Aries subjects were prone to headaches, but the article said nothing about being prone to heartache!

It was her own fault for having a late March birthday. Everyone knew Arians charged at their problems like the proverbial bull in a china shop. In future, she would be more like the calm, collected district nurse she was supposed to be. She couldn't do anything to prevent Craig from marrying Lyn. The only way she could salvage her pride was to pretend that she didn't care. If she cast up Alec's name every now and again, and pretended to visit him, no one would guess her secret.

Christmas wasn't far off, and Rosemary spared a thought for those of her patients who were alone. Granny Cole was number one on her list, but getting to her wasn't that easy. The cart-track had, as she had suspected, become a mire, so she left the car and walked, her green country wellies squelching at every step.

Mrs Cole had just recovered from a bout of bronchitis, but seemed happy enough. Rosemary stayed longer than she intended. The old lady was so welcoming, so full of country courtesy that it made each visit a pleasure.

'Lyn's been to see me,' was the old lady's parting sentence when at length Rosemary tore herself away.

'I'm so glad!' Impulsively, Rosemary kissed Granny's brow. Then she realised—Lyn must have put the family feud to one side so she could tell her grandmother of her conquest: she was to be the doctor's wife.

Rosemary didn't stop to ask questions, because she had already supplied her own answers.

After a hectic day, she was glad to get home. Spike was all over her, as usual, and she buried her face in his fur. It was softer now, and there was more of it, the unsightly patchiness having grown over. He was the only creature who loved her, she felt, even though she knew she was being melodramatic. Her Aunt Lizzie loved her, so did some of the older patients. She had at long last been accepted, even by those who bitterly resented 'furriners'. To them, that meant anyone who hadn't lived in Sussex for at least thirty years!

Life in Hurstfield would be good in the summer months. She could take Spike for long walks in the Forest . . .

She frowned. He seemed to want his walk now, but she'd already let him into the garden. He kept going to the front door and pawing the ground, before gazing at her. Then Rosemary saw the envelope.

She bent to pick it up, and Spike whined. It must have been there when she arrived home. Yes, there was her footmark on what had once been an expensive white envelope.

Quickly she tore it open. Craig Dean's writing was unmistakable, even though the envelope bore only the words 'For Rosemary'.

Then she regretted her haste in opening it, and hesitated before finally plucking up the courage to read the words she dreaded. It wasn't, thank goodness, a wedding invitation, but that might yet come.

No, Craig wouldn't be so insensitive. Yet he might invite her and Alec together; he wasn't to know that she had lied about loving Alec.

She had to read it twice before she really took it in. The note was brief, and shouldn't have been that difficult to understand. Craig was taking her out to dinner, and could she please be ready by seven-thirty. He would try not to be late. There was a postscript. 'Glad rags', he had written.

Glad rags for him, perhaps. All Rosemary wanted was a set of mourning clothes! Nevertheless, she had no thought of turning down the invitation. It was their last chance to be alone.

She couldn't believe there was a restaurant within easy driving distance that was worth dressing up for. Then she remembered the Country Club. It was an old mansion which had been turned into a hotel and country club, and which lay to the north of the Forest. Perhaps he was taking her there.

Despite the bitter cold of the late afternoon, Rosemary took Spike for an extra long walk first, letting him loose on the Common, for a change. It was risky, since he didn't always come when called, but he was to be left most of the evening, and that made her feel guilty.

It was dark and lonely on the Common, and Rosemary cursed her impetuous nature for the umpteenth time. Arians were reckless, she mentally added to the magazine article—they needed firm handling!

Spike wouldn't come when she first called, and, alarmed, she went in search of him. She shone the powerful torch, and the light picked up not only the dog but also a woman. It was someone Spike knew, for he was prancing around her.

Rosemary called again, and this time Spike obeyed, greeting Rosemary with his deep-throated baying. She didn't recognise Spike's companion at first, muffled up as she was in hooded anorak, headscarf and trousers. Then the newcomer pushed back her hood, and Rosemary saw that it was Sarah Spilstead, the teenage daughter of one of her patients.

'I thought it was your dog, Sister,' the girl said shyly. 'I was just having a little walk—I don't get enough exercise, my mum says,' she added defensively, as though expecting criticism for leaving her terminally-ill mother.

Rosemary knew that Sarah, barely seventeen, carried most of the burden of caring for her widowed mother. The only other child was a boy of thirteen, who apparently spent all his free time out with his mates. Sarah knew of the seriousness of her mother's illness, but Mrs Spilstead was adamant that the boy wasn't to be told—a decision Rosemary respected but disagreed with.

There was no more nursing to be carried out, but the whole primary care team tried to support cancer sufferers and their relatives, if possible. They were all concerned about the burden young Sarah carried. At seventeen, she ought to be going to dances, meeting boys, having a good time. Before she knew it, she would be in her twenties and bitterly regretting her lost opportunities.

Rosemary encouraged Sarah to come back with them. She was mindful of the time, yet couldn't let the girl wander aimlessly about by herself in the dark. Rosemary hadn't brought the car, so all three ran most of the way back to her cottage. She intended driving Sarah home, then hurrying back to change—Craig mustn't be kept waiting.

Sarah looked so poorly that Rosemary had to revise her plans. It was nearly seven, and she still had to bath and change, yet she couldn't let the girl go without a snack and a cup of coffee.

Sarah tucked into the scratch meal so heartily that Rosemary wondered what she ate at home. 'Your mother is still having a light diet, I expect?' she threw in casually, and Sarah nodded between mouthfuls of meat pasty.

'Some days she just drinks. Other times she feels like a bit of fish,' she affirmed.

'So if she's on a non-eating day, you don't bother to cook for yourself?'

Sarah coloured. 'I have to get tea for my brother when he comes home from school, but he just eats bread and jam or baked beans. He gets dinner at school and I always give him crisps or cake for break-time.'

It sounded as if neither child was eating properly, though school dinners were fairly nutritious. A case for the social worker, Rosemary felt, and one she would mention to Dr Tunstall, who was the Spilsteads' doctor.

By the time a happier Sarah was ready to leave, it was gone seven-thirty, and there was no sign of Craig. Rosemary rang him at home, but there was no reply. She listened to the ringing tone, her thoughts far from happy. Had he forgotten the invitation, or was he out on a call? And, more important, where was Lyn?

She replaced the receiver, then summoned up a smile for Sarah. 'Come on, I'll give you a lift home. Spike can come as well.'

'You look sad, Sister,' the girl commented. 'I suppose even doctors and nurses have problems, too.'

Rosemary's smile broadened. 'Yes, I'm afraid we do! Still, my problem is much smaller than yours—it will keep for now.' Her heart aching, she slammed the front door behind them, half hoping the phone would ring, but it did not.

Mrs Spilstead was definitely weaker, and Rosemary promised to look in on her again the next day. She had pain-killers, of course, and assured Rosemary that the pain was under control, but this was an aspect of her care that needed further investigation, Rosemary felt. Mrs Spilstead was still able to dress each day, but felt too weak to assist with the housework, apart from dusting, and laying the table for whatever meal she fancied. Sarah carried out the remainder of the household duties, as her mother was adamant about not wanting a home help.

It was an enormous problem, and one Rosemary intended to solve. It would help to take her mind off the forthcoming marriage, anyway. She hadn't seen as much of Mrs Spilstead as she would have wished, with the whooping cough cases taking up so much time, but now she could remedy that.

If Rosemary hoped she would find Craig's car parked outside her cottage on her return, she was out of luck. It was far too late for him to come now, but she went through the motions of getting ready anyway, more to cheer herself up than from any expectation that he would visit. She knew she was being foolish, but at least there was no one to witness her foolishness, except Spike.

She had intended giving Craig the works tonight —eye-shadow, glitter mascara, the lot! So, after her bath, she carefully made up her face, using the wickedly green eye-shadow that lent colour to her grey eyes.

She hadn't given much thought to what she would wear, though her choice was limited, anyway. Frowning, she decided against the deep pink, which Craig had seen before. That left either the navy, which he had also seen, or the little black number. As she found that she couldn't get into the little black number, the problem was solved for her!

She was just zipping herself into the navy dress when the doorbell rang. Spike barked, then began to scratch at the door, his powerful tail thudding against it.

It must be Craig. Rosemary glanced down at her dress, feeling stupid for dressing up when Craig clearly wouldn't be taking her out this evening. It was getting on for ten, and she hurried downstairs, half dreading whatever message he was bringing.

The bell rang again as she got there, and she opened the door to face a very angry Craig Dean.

'What in hell's name are you up to?' he snapped, before Rosemary could greet him. 'I've been searching everywhere for you!'

He gripped her wrists and began to shake her, releasing her only when a protective Spike growled.

'Perhaps you ought to come in,' she said tightly. 'It won't do your image much good if the neighbours see us quarrelling on the doorstep!'

Craig controlled himself with a visible effort. 'Doctors and nurses have problems too, Rosemary. It wouldn't hurt the public to realise that—instead of putting us on a pedestal!'

Rosemary counted to ten, then carefully closed the front door. 'The GP is a minor god, and the nursing sister is an angel!' she murmured, her sense of humour surfacing again.

Craig's eyes were cool as they rested on her. 'I'm no god, and you're no angel, that's for sure. Where the hell *were* you?'

'Out with Spike.' Rosemary did not embroider the statement. Why should she answer to Craig for what she did when she was off duty? She never knew what *he* was up to!

'Rosemary—*where were you?*' Craig's voice was as cold as his eyes, and he half rose from the settee.

Her eyes widened. 'I—I took Spike out for a run on the Common. Then I met one of Dr Tunstall's patients, so I brought her back here for a snack and——'

'All right, I'm sorry I asked. Spare me the details!'

'You were asking for the details a moment ago!' Rosemary pointed out tartly. Then her anger faded and she crossed swiftly to his side. 'Craig—I'm sorry,' she said simply. 'I didn't mean to quarrel with you.'

'You shouldn't bring patients back here, Rosemary. Off-duty time is supposed to be for forgetting patients,' he said gently.

'I know, but I feel so sorry for the girl! Her mother is terminal, and——'

'Rosemary, try not to carry your nursing problems over into your off duty. It doesn't help the patient if we become too emotionally involved,' Craig pointed out quietly, and Rosemary knew he was right. 'Perhaps the nursing sister *is* an angel, after all!' he mused. Then his quizzical glance took in the sophisticated navy dress, the evening sandals, the full-scale make-up. 'I see you're all dressed for an evening out. Could it be with me, I wonder?'

Rosemary pretended to frown. 'It *might* be for your benefit, doctor. I really couldn't say.'

She was overjoyed to hear Craig chuckle. 'It's rather late for dinner now, Sister Miller. I'm sorry I wasn't here promptly—I had a baby to deliver. How about tomorrow night? Let's make it a celebration dinner, shall we?' His voice was teasing.

Rosemary's expression was reproachful. 'I didn't know we had anything to celebrate, doctor. Shouldn't you be getting back home to your fiancée?' How could he be so thoughtless? He must realise that she cared for him, surely?

'Aunt Lizzie didn't spank you often enough when you were younger,' he said sternly. 'It isn't too late, though.' He reached for her, and she squealed.

'No, Craig! I——' Her words of protest were cut off as their lips met.

Spike, thinking it was a game, jumped on the settee beside Rosemary, and reluctantly she left the sanctuary of Craig's embrace. Good old Spike, she thought; he had probably saved her from admitting her love for Craig. This time there would have been no drawing back—their love sought the final consummation. It was thanks to Spike that she still had some vestiges of self-respect.

Craig smiled lazily, and Rosemary's determination wavered. She swayed towards him again, as if drawn by an invisible thread, but to her chagrin he rose, and went over to stand by the fire.

'I'd better go, Sister Miller,' he said softly, 'or I shan't be able to keep you at arm's length until our wedding!'

Rosemary stared blankly. '*What* wedding? You're marrying Lyn!' she cried.

Craig looked mystified. 'Am I? I once told you I didn't love her.'

'But—all the time you've spent with her! All the plans you've been making!' she wailed, wondering if it was all some crazy dream and that she would shortly awake. 'Why, I saw you and Lyn talking to the vicar last Sunday!'

'*And* Lyn's husband,' Craig put in. 'Didn't you see him, Rosemary?' He came nearer, and kissed the tip of her nose, before retreating to the fireside again. 'All this time I've been holding Lyn together,' he went on slowly. 'She needs someone strong to lean on—she's one of the broken reeds of this world. She really loves Peter, though I doubt if she fully realises that. Steve needs his father, anyway.'

'Despite calling you "Daddy Craig",' Rosemary put in gently.

He frowned. 'That was Lyn's doing, the boy told me himself. Yet I couldn't tell her off, and I couldn't, until recently, admit to her that I loved you. I needed to get her problems sorted out first, then I intended to concentrate on *you*. She would have turned her evil temper on you, if she'd known about our love.' He hesitated, then went on: 'I once believed I loved her, but that was a long time ago. It's over now. She and Peter are together, and they've left the Forest. I can't say I'm sorry.'

'When—when you kissed me once, you called me "Lyn". Perhaps you *do* still love her, just a little?' Rosemary's voice was wistful as she recalled the day she had spent nursing Craig after his bout of 'flu.

He chuckled. 'I knew I was kissing the shapely Sister Miller! I pretended to be feverish so I could have a cuddle—without you pushing me away!'

'You used to kiss her,' Rosemary went on stubbornly. 'I *saw* you. In the *surgery*, of all places!'

'Lyn kissed *me*, I seem to remember, and it was solely for your benefit. Now, where was I?'

'I believe you were about to propose, doctor!' said Rosemary, with an impish smile.

'More of an order than a proposal, Sister Miller,' Craig said sternly, moving towards her, and this time Spike didn't object as Rosemary melted into his arms.

Her last coherent thought was that they would have a new home, though Craig didn't know it yet. The house she had so often admired was up for sale, and she knew Craig would love the friendly old house as much as she did—and Spike would adore the garden!

Mills & Boon

YOU'RE INVITED TO ACCEPT
4 DOCTOR NURSE
ROMANCES
AND A TOTE BAG

 # FREE!

Doctor Nurse ————

Acceptance card

| NO STAMP
NEEDED | Post to: **Reader Service, FREEPOST,**
P.O. Box 236, Croydon, Surrey. CR9 9EL |

Please note readers in Southern Africa write to:
Independant Book Services P.T.Y., Postbag X3010, Randburg 2125, S. Africa

YES! Please send me 4 free Doctor Nurse Romances
and my free tote bag – and reserve a Reader
Service Subscription for me. If I decide to subscribe I shall
receive 6 new Doctor Nurse Romances every other month as
soon as they come off the presses for £6.60 together with a
FREE newsletter including information on top authors and
special offers, exclusively for Reader Service subscribers.
There are no postage and packing charges, and I understand I
may cancel or suspend my subscription at any time. If I decide
not to subscribe I shall write to you within 10 days. Even if I
decide not to subscribe the 4 free novels and the tote bag are
mine to keep forever. I am over 18 years of age   EP23D

NAME ——————————————————————
                                    (CAPITALS PLEASE)

ADDRESS ——————————————————————

————————————————————————————

———————————————— POSTCODE ——————